groucho Marx,
Master Detective

groucho Marx,
Master Detective

Ron Goulart

St. Martin's Press
New York

Production Editor: David Stanford Burr

Library of Congress Cataloging-in-Publication Data

Goulart, Ron
  Groucho Marx, master detective / Ron Goulart. — 1st ed.
    p. cm.
  "A Thomas Dunne book."
  ISBN 0-312-18106—X
  1. Marx, Groucho, 1891–1977—Fiction. I. Title.
  PS3557.085G76   1998
  813'.54—dc21   97–31393
               CIP

First edition: April 1998

10 9 8 7 6 5 4 3 2 1

To Ivy Fischer Stone, full-time agent and part-time muse

Acknowledgment

I appreciate the cooperation of Robert A. Finkelstein of Groucho Marx Productions.

groucho Marx,
Master Detective

One

The world wasn't in especially great shape that autumn of 1937. And I ought to know, I was there.

Hitler was quite obviously already warming up for World War II, the Japanese were moving across China and there was civil war in Spain. America was suffering a recession and workers were staging sit-down strikes all across the country. The Prince of Wales had renounced his throne for the woman he loved, John D. Rockefeller had died, Amelia Earhart had gone missing in the Pacific.

In Hollywood Groucho Marx solved his first murder case.

Very few people were ever aware that Groucho carried on a successful sideline as an amateur detective. But from the late 1930s, trust me, Groucho was giving such West Coast sleuths as Philip Marlowe, Sam Spade and Dan Turner some stiff competition. A well-read and perceptive fellow, Groucho turned out to have a real affinity for investigating and solving crimes. "My sleuthing turned Sherlock Holmes green with envy," he once mentioned. "Or maybe that was only because we left him out in the rain too long."

I served him as a sort of Dr. Watson for most of his career "I don't need anybody to scribble down accounts of these capers," he told me after we'd been at this for a while. "If you were a real doctor, though, you might be able to tell me why I feel so tearful and forlorn whenever the first of the month rolls around. You could also explain these strange greenish spots people report seeing on my backside."

My name is Frank Denby and I wasn't yet a screenwriter at that point. I'd been a police reporter for the *Los Angeles Times* until early in 1936 and then quit to turn out radio scripts.

Don't worry, by the way, that this account is not going to star Groucho. I learned a long time ago that whether people loved him—which a lot of them did—or hated him—and there were, believe me, quite a few of them, too—they were always more interested in Groucho than they were in me. He'll be making a typical Groucho entrance shortly, but first I want to get some of the details about me out of the way, so that you'll understand how I came to be the Boswell of Julius Marx all those years ago.

His first real detective case got going on a bright, clear morning in October 1937. Groucho was approaching his late forties. A few months earlier MGM's *A Day at the Races,* in which he starred with his brothers Harpo and Chico, had opened across America to mixed reviews but a very impressive box office take.

I was just shy of thirty and living alone since my divorce the year before, in a small ramshackle beach cottage in the Southern California town of Bayside. My wife quit me a few weeks after I'd quit the paper.

I met Jane Danner on that particular autumn morning. She became the love of my life, but neither one of us had any notion that we were going to spend the rest of our days together.

I was driving a secondhand Plymouth coupe in those days. The previous owner had painted it a bright lemon yellow and attached an imitation raccoon tail to the radio antenna. I had to be in Beverly Hills for a meeting at an ad agency at ten A.M. that morning and I left my place a little before nine.

Groucho was going to be at that meeting, too.

When I turned onto Oceanside Boulevard the car radio was playing "Bei Mir Bist Du Schon," the Andrews Sisters hit that I'd already heard several dozen times so far that week.

"You know," I said aloud—I tend to talk to myself quite a lot, so be prepared—"I still don't have any idea what those lyrics mean."

Traffic up ahead seemed unusually thick and tangled.

"I wonder if even the Andrews Sisters know."

I heard a siren now.

About a block ahead was a large wedge of vehicles blocking most of my side of the wide boulevard. There were three Bayside Police Department cars parked in the street at assorted odd angles and another one up on the dry narrow lawn of a small stucco cottage.   .

A dusty white ambulance shared the patch of lawn with the police car and a second ambulance was just roaring to a stop on the sidewalk. Several other cars were parked on both street and sidewalk and more were pulling up. Three uniformed cops were trying to keep back a gaggle of what looked to be reporters and photographers. From this distance I couldn't recognize any of my former colleagues. They seemed to be interested in the small garage attached to the cottage.

Suddenly a new police car shot in front of me from the left.

"Jesus!" I swung the Plymouth's steering wheel hard to the right, hitting the gas pedal.

My car lurched, getting out of the way about five seconds short of getting sideswiped.

I started to sigh, then stopped.

From my right came an odd rattling noise, then a woman's cry and then more rattling.

I hit the brakes. Pulling on the emergency, I shifted into neutral and hopped free of the car. On the radio the announcer was delivering a commercial for a bargain funeral home.

I hurried around the front of the yellow car.

"Are you okay?" I asked.

An auburn-haired young woman, very pretty, wearing a tweed skirt and a green cardigan, was sitting on the pavement with her bare legs spread wide. A bicycle, looking out of kilter and surreal, lay nearby.

"What was the question?" she asked.

"Are you hurt? Did I hit you?"

She looked up at me. "No, I hit you I believe."·

"Well, that was because I had to swerve to avoid getting smacked by the damn cop car."

"That sounds plausible."

"The more important inquiry has to do with what shape you're in. Especially your bones and such."

"Help me up." She held out a hand. "And we'll run a few tests."

I took her hand and, somehow, felt a mild electric shock. That was when I started to fall in love with Jane Danner and I came to understand the Prince of Wales. If I'd had a throne, it would have been given up right then and there.

She wiggled her left foot, then her right. Wiggled each hand in turn. "I seem to be shipshape." Leaning to the right, she looked around me and at her fallen bike. "But my bicycle's all askew, isn't it?"

"Afraid so. Can I deliver you someplace?"

"That would be nice."

I opened the rumble seat of my Plymouth, gathered up the injured bike and managed to get it stowed away. "Where were you going?"

"To work—about a mile from here. On Palm Lane."

"Sure, that's right on my way," I told her. "Well, even if it weren't, I'd get you there. I'll buy you a new bike, too."

"To keep me from suing you for everything you possess?"

"That's one good reason, yeah. But I happen to be a chivalrous fellow and anytime I knock a girl off a bike and damage it, I replace the damn thing."

"Fine by me." Hands on hips, she was surveying the traffic jam that was growing down the block. "Any idea what the heck is going on?"

"Something serious I'd guess. A death probably."

"Actress," said a middle-aged newsboy from the sidewalk. He was wearing a long tan overcoat and had a bundle of morning newspapers tucked up under his right arm. "Lived up there. Did the Dutch."

"Suicide, huh?" I said.

"Yep, so they're saying."

Nodding, I opened the passenger door. "My name's Frank Denby."

"I'm Jane Danner." She slid into my coupe. "Are you currently married?"

After coming around and getting in, I answered, "Divorced. You?"

"Haven't been married so far. Engaged three times, though."

I eased the car around the vehicles that blocked the way and turned onto a side street. "Is that a pattern?"

"So far, yes. I tend to leave them at the altar."

I asked, "What sort of job am I taking you to?"

"It's kind of odd."

"Oh, so?"

Rising up on our right was a huge billboard advertising *Lost Horizon* with Ronald Colman.

"Ever heard of a comic strip called *Hillbilly Willie?*"

"Sure, everybody has. Rod Tommerlin draws it and it runs locally in the *Examiner.*"

"Well, I help draw it."

"Do you draw the outhouses?"

"Right, and most of the pigs and mules."

"I like those outhouses. Especially the little crescent moons cut in the doors."

"I take it, Frank—judging from the slightly snide tone I'm sensing here—that you yourself do something far loftier than mountain boy humor."

"Nope. I write radio shows actually," I informed her as we turned back onto Oceanview.

"What? Soap operas like *Ma Perkins?* Or funny stuff like *Jack Benny?*"

"I've done both sorts of shows. Most recently I wrote a detective show called *Crime Reporter.* Chester Morris did that one for a season, but we didn't get renewed," I said. "I'm back with comedy now, working on a new show called *Groucho Marx, Master Detective.*"

"Oh, I love the Marx Brothers. I thought *Duck Soup* was the funniest—"

"This is just Groucho. Something he can do on his own until they decide whether they're going to do another movie."

"I hope they will. Harpo's my favorite. He's cute."

"Cute, but difficult to fit into a radio format," I observed. "Matter of fact, I'm on my way to a meeting with the ad agency we're doing the show for. Going to be a network guy there, too. And Groucho will probably show up, if he remembers."

"What's he like?"

"Well, he doesn't have a moustache in real life."

"I've heard that, yes," Jane said. "Oh, by the way, you passed Palm Lane two blocks back."

"Oops." I pulled to the curb, checked the rearview mirror and then executed a U-turn. "You busy tonight?"

"I'm free any time after six."

"Okay, I'll arrive shortly after six and we'll go to dinner. Okay?"

"Fine. I live at 2303 Mar Vista Way."

"Not too far from my place."

"Walk over, then, and we can try a favorite bistro of mine on the beach."

I drove in silence for a few seconds, then said, "This has been an unusual morning for me."

Jane smiled. "Wait till you see what the evening's going to be like."

Two

The offices of the Pauker, Hatton & Underwood advertising agency occupied an entire floor in a brand-new building on Wilshire Boulevard on the edge of Beverly Hills. The senior meeting room was done up in extreme art deco style and everything in it was either stark white or dense black.

When I got there, about fifteen minutes late, three of the eight black chairs around the white oval table were already occupied. Jape Griffin, the large wide sunbrown account man on the Orem Bros. Coffee account, sat at the head of the table. Warren Stander, a small weary man in his fifties, was a vice president for programming at the Nationwide Broadcasting Network and had placed himself as far from Jape as possible. Jape's secretary—I was pretty sure her first name was either Betty or Betsy but had no notion as to her last name—was seated at her boss's right hand. There was a copy of the latest draft of my radio script at each place and as a centerpiece a pyramid rose, made of ten of the familiar gold and blue Orem Bros. Coffee cans.

"You must think you're Groucho," observed Jape as I sat down.

"Hm?"

"You're fourteen minutes late," said the account executive. "Of course, he's not here yet."

Pointing at one of the windows, I explained, "I got tangled in traffic."

Making a grunting noise, Jape picked up his copy of the script. "The client, that's Junior Orem, isn't completely happy about the title of our proposed show, Frank."

"What's he unhappy about? And how come a guy who's near seventy is still known as Junior?"

"He feels that *Groucho Marx, Master Detective* is too bland."

"It's supposed to be ironic."

"Irony doesn't sell coffee." He patted his blond secretary on the arm. "Betsy."

She smiled across at me and flipped open her steno book. "Mr. Orem suggests *Groucho Marx, Silly Detective. Groucho Marx, Screwball Detective. Groucho Marx of the Famous Marx Bros. Joins Forces with Deeply Satisfying Orem Bros. Coffee to Bring You Goofy Mysteries Every Week.*"

"Oh, I love that last one," I said, slumping in my black chair and producing a believable groan. "It has zing and is, furthermore, streamlined. Jesus, Jape."

"You're eventually going to have to capitulate to the client's wishes."

"Yeah, but it'll take fifteen minutes just to read that damned title. Leaving only fifteen for the whole show and the commercials."

"If I were a writer—which, praise be, I'm not—I'd sit up and pay attention when a client told me my title was dull and drab," Jape told me.

"You're thinking of my laundry, not my script. And it isn't dull and drab—not since I switched to Rinso." I held up both hands. "And I got rid of my dishpan hands, too."

Jape patted his secretary's arm again.

She turned to a new page in the steno book. "The client is also perturbed by the suspicion that both the proposed writer and the proposed star of the radio show are making snide remarks about him behind his back. Furthermore—"

"Did I miss the sermon?" A middle-sized man with an impressive tennis court tan came rushing into the meeting room, crouching slightly. He was wearing a checked sport coat, a tan polo shirt and slacks of a russet hue.

"Sit down, Groucho," suggested Jape. "This concerns you."

Groucho Marx gazed around the black and white room. "Too bad you couldn't afford Technicolor." Circling the white oval table, he stopped next to Betsy and tugged a small purplish bouquet from inside his coat. "Orchids for you, my pet."

She, reluctantly, accepted the flowers, nose wrinkling. "These aren't orchids, Mr. Marx. They look like petunias to me."

"I thought two bouquets for a quarter was too good a price for South American orchids." He continued around and dropped into the seat next to me. "Have you been defending our honor, Rollo?"

"To the best of my ability, sir."

Stander spoke now. His voice was dry and rasping. "Can

we assume that the clowning is over and we can get down to business at last?"

Groucho checked his gold wristwatch. "Actually, Warren, the clowning isn't scheduled to commence for another half hour yet," he explained. "What you've been enjoying up to now has been the overture as rendered by an all male choir—and that should tickle your fancy. What have they been bitching about, Franklin?"

"The title of our radio show," I told him. "Seems the client finds it dull and dingy."

"The title," said Groucho, standing up and pointing a finger at the white ceiling, "happens to be the best title I have ever heard for a radio show. It brings tears to the eyes—or maybe that's just the onions you had for breakfast, Warren. Be that as it may, the title is terrific." He sat down again, tugged a second bouquet from out of his coat and tossed it across to Betsy. "And keep in mind, Jape dear, that I've worked with some of the most brilliant writers of the century. George Kaufman, Arthur Sheekman, Morrie Ryskind, Sid Perelman, George Bernard Shaw, Harry Ruby and—"

"When the hell did you work with George Bernard Shaw?" inquired Jape.

"Oh, that's right," said Groucho, "he never finished the script he was working on for us. His whiskers kept getting tangled up in the typewriter keys. Broke his heart and caused him to become a vegetarian. If the title goes, we go." He settled back in the chair and produced a cigar out of his breast pocket.

"There are," put in the NBN executive, "other problems."

"Give us an example, Little Eva," invited Groucho, as he lit his cigar with a wood match.

"We're not going to be able to okay the name you've chosen for the detective you're going to play on this show."

"Why, pray tell?"

"It's lewd and lowbrow. J. Hawkshaw Transom." Stander tapped thin fingers on the script. "Suggestive of cheap hotels and smutty assignations."

"Gee, I never caught that until now." He exhaled smoke and nudged me. "That's what I get for working with this youthful offender here." Suddenly he lunged and grabbed one of the Orem Bros. Coffee cans from the bottom row. "Here's something else I never noticed until just now."

The pyramid of cans went toppling. One rolled into Betsy's lap, another sailed over the edge of the white table and thunked onto the black carpeting.

"One of the Orem boys has a glass eye." Groucho had the can close to his face and was frowning at the engraved portraits of the three founding Orem brothers. "Doesn't match the other one at all. And just think, Rollo, I've been swilling down this stuff every morn for—what is it? three weeks now—and never spotted this." He tapped the can. "What this is is one of those glass eyes they use in stuffing chipmunks." He thrust the can toward me. "See?"

"I'd say it's a squirrel eye."

"You think so? No, squirrels usually look smarter and more honest than that."

Jape put in, "Groucho, we're supposed to go on the air with your new radio show in less than two weeks. If we can't get together with the client and the network on these minor changes—well, we may have to drop the project."

"That's okay by me. I have an offer to work as a prioress down in Tijuana. Pays better than this halfwit show and I don't have to drink anybody's vile coffee." He popped to his feet, took a few slouching steps toward the door. Then he halted, smacked his forehead and returned. Scowling down at the white table, he said, "The last time I saw a table like this, there was somebody being dissected on top of it." He put a paternal hand on my shoulder. "I just realized I can't leave this poor lad in the lurch—especially since his lurch is in such pathetic shape. All rusty and covered with those odd little bumps."

"Can we," requested Jape, "get back to the script?"

"The script is perfect as it is." Groucho sat, took a puff of his cigar. "I might go so far as to say it is the most brilliant and hilarious script I have ever had the pleasure to read. I might even go so far as Pasadena if my folks will let me borrow the car tonight." Leaning closer to me, he whispered, "The rewrite is okay, isn't it? I haven't had time to look at it."

"You were right the first time," I assured him. "It is brilliant."

"Then screw these bastards. We'll stand our ground. Although J. Hawkshaw Transom is a lousy name."

"Not lousy, mediocre at worst. But in the tradition of most of your movie names," I reminded him. "Dr. Hugo Z. Hackenbush, Otis B. Driftwood, Waldorf J. Flywheel, etc."

"True," he admitted. "By the way, Rollo, you look strangely elated this morning—it can't be this godawful get-together."

"I'm pretty sure I fell head over heels in love about an hour and a half ago."

Smiling, Groucho leaned back, exhaled smoke and rubbed his hands together. "Ah, splendid," he said, "I'll do my best to screw that up for you."

Three

There was a warm wind drifting in across the darkening Pacific.

Jane and I were holding hands by the time we left the Neptune Café. The electric shocks had subsided for the most part.

She wore a simple pale green dress and her reddish hair was held back by a single twist of black ribbon. "Usually their clam chowder has clams in it," she was explaining. "Tonight was an exception."

"Everything was great," I assured her.

We began walking slowly along the twilight beach, heading for my humble cottage.

"I suppose I ought to warn you," she said.

"That you're eventually going to abandon me on the church steps?"

"No, not at all," she told me, laughing. "What I'm feeling is that you're going to be the exception."

"Did I mention that I got an electric shock the first time I touched you?"

"Irish witches on my mother's side."

The day continued to fade and by the time we reached my weathered cottage darkness had closed in.

Jane stopped. "Is that your house yonder?"

"The one that looks like Hillbilly Willie's homestead, yeah."

"Well, there's somebody lurking on your porch."

I narrowed my eyes. "That's a familiar silhouette." I guided her onto the cracked flagstone path that cut up across my sparse front yard. "Groucho?"

"I telephoned twice, Frank, but didn't get an answer," said the actor from the shadowy porch. "I decided to drop over. I want to talk to you about something."

"This is Jane Danner," I said when we reached the porch. "I was telling you about her."

"Pleased to meet you, Mr. Marx. Telling you what?"

"The lad is completely smitten, Miss Danner." Groucho shook her hand and bowed slightly. He was carrying a folded copy of the *Los Angeles Times* under his arm. "I hate to interrupt you kids, but this is important."

"That's okay." I located my key and unlocked the front door.

"Smitten, huh?" Jane said to Groucho.

He nodded. "Head over heels was how he put it. And I'd say he had good reason."

A large flowered sofa and two matching armchairs crowded my small living room. The pair of matching floor lamps had parchment shades depicting sailboats in the sunset. A husky radio sat in a corner.

"Place came furnished," I informed everybody after turning on the overhead light. "My wife got our real furniture when—"

"It's very quaint," said Jane.

Groucho crossed to an armchair, sat and tapped the folded newspaper on his knee. "I need your help, Frank."

"This doesn't have anything to do with our radio show, does it?" I sat myself on the sofa, facing the actor.

"Nothing at all, no." From an inner pocket of his sport coat he extracted a pair of rimless reading glasses. He put them on and opened the *Times* to a middle page. "Somebody called me about this a couple hours ago." He coughed into his hand, adjusted the glasses, looked away from the paper for a few seconds. "It's this little story here in the middle of the page, about Peg McMorrow. 'STARLET TAKES LIFE. DESPONDENT YOUNG ACTRESS A SUICIDE.' "

"That's the girl this morning." Jane sat next to me and touched my hand. "I meant to tell you."

Groucho took off his glasses and stared at the two of us. "You know something about Peg's death?"

"Not exactly. But that's what caused the traffic tie-up this morning."

"Which is how we met," continued Jane. "Everything was all tangled up in the vicinity of her cottage, Mr. Marx. You know, police cars, ambulances, reporters, gawkers and all that. At the time we didn't know exactly who had died, but somebody did say an actress had killed herself."

I was watching Groucho. "You knew her, obviously."

Standing up, he tossed the paper to the faded carpet. "Two years ago I . . ." Groucho rubbed his knuckle under his nose and began pacing. "Let's say we were good friends for several months back in 1935. Peg—Christ, Peg would only be twenty-two now. She was twenty, fresh from Iola, Wisconsin, of all places. She was pretty, bright . . ." He shrugged. "Not a bad actress either." He moved to the window and looked out across the beach toward the dark ocean. "I haven't seen Peg since then, but I've more or less kept up with her. Abe Bockman's been her agent for over a year and I run into him fairly often at the Hillcrest Country Club. A real schmuck, but a passable agent."

I asked, "How exactly can I help you?"

Turning his back on the night sea, Groucho replied, "Peg would never have killed herself."

"Anybody can commit suicide. Dying is easy."

"No, not Peg. She wasn't that kind of—"

"Two years, Mr. Marx. That's a long time ago," Jane said. "People change."

Groucho went over and picked up the fallen newspaper. "This rag quotes her suicide note. She supposedly said she was depressed because her career wasn't going anywhere."

"People kill themselves for lesser reasons than that," I pointed out.

"I ran into Abe only last week and he told me Peg was about to sign a three-year contract with Paragon Pictures."

Jane suggested, "Maybe that deal fell through."

"I don't think so."

"Have you talked to Abe Bockman since you heard about her death?"

"I tried, but his secretary informed me he's up in Frisco on some deal and can't be reached," said Groucho. "I'll tell you something else, kids. They found Peg in her garage, slumped in the front seat of her little coupe. They claim she sealed up the garage and sat in the car with the motor running until she died." He shook his head. "Peg had a bad case of claustrophobia. She'd never lock herself inside a small space like that—not even to kill herself."

I was frowning. "Wait now, Groucho," I said slowly. "Peg McMorrow is dead and you don't believe she killed herself. That doesn't leave many other possibilities. Chiefly accident or murder."

Groucho lowered himself into the armchair. "Somebody killed her."

"What's the motive?"

"I don't know. Not yet."

"Was she involved with somebody who might have—"

"I'm going to find out."

Jane asked, "Why is this so important to you, Mr. Marx?"

He looked at her and then up at the peach-colored ceiling. "That's a very pertinent question, Miss Danner," he answered finally. "I have to tell you that I'm not exactly certain. Could be I'm getting sentimental as I dodder into middle age." He paused, took out a cigar. He put it in his mouth but made no attempt to light it. "What I am sure of is that I have a very strong feeling that something's wrong here." He pointed at the newspaper. "For instance, you saw reporters flocking around this morning. And think about this—a pretty young actress dies mysteriously. That's headline stuff, yet not one of the newspapers hereabouts paid much attention to the story. All of them buried it."

"A coverup?" I asked.

"We'll find out," promised Groucho. "You used to handle the crime beat, right?"

"For the *Times* for nearly six years."

20

"I want to see copies of all the police reports on this, I want to know what the coroner has to say," Groucho told me. "Pictures, too, and any reporters' notes you can get hold of. For details on Peg's private life and her career I have contacts of my own."

"The Bayside police," I mentioned, "are not the most honest and forthright in the land. And lots of them don't like outsiders and amateurs nosing around."

"Bribe somebody if you have to."

"No, I know a few relatively honest cops I can talk to. I still have a contact with someone who can get us the medical stuff."

Groucho said, "I also want to find her body."

Jane sat up straight. "Is it missing?"

"I'm thinking of taking care of the funeral if nobody else does. She didn't have much in the way of next of kin."

"Just phone the authorities and—"

"Did that," said Groucho. "I got the run-around."

I scratched at my chin. "That *is* kind of funny," I said. "I'll find out about that, too."

Groucho said, "Can you start right now?"

"Sure," I told him.

He glanced from me to Jane. "Over the years I've realized that I have a real knack for detective work," he said. "Why, back during my vaudeville days, I was the one who found out who shot Ginsburg the Human Cannon Ball." Shoulders slouching, he began to pace on my threadbare imitation Persian rug. "Nobody much liked Ginsburg, because he was always going off half cocked. Still, as Ben Franklin so wisely put it, half a—Ah, but I shouldn't be jesting at a time like this."

"You're using humor to hide your true feelings of grief and sorrow," Jane told him.

Groucho stopped still, straightening up. "Jove, this woman is absolutely brilliant." He leaped clean over the coffee table and grabbed her hand up out of her lap. He did a deep bow and kissed it several times. Then he looked at me and added, "Get rid of her at the earliest opportunity, Rollo. Brilliant women can ruin a chap."

Taking back her hand, Jane asked me, "Are you going to help him, Frank?"

I'd already made up my mind on that one. "Yeah, with a detective like him and a reporter like me— Hell, we ought to be able to solve this." I nodded at Groucho. "You're sure you want to go ahead with this—no matter what we turn up."

"I want to find the bastard who killed her," he said evenly.

I held out my hand. "Then you've got an assistant."

"You're a good lad, Rollo." After shaking hands, he reached up and patted me on the head. "By the way, before all this started for me I got around to reading your rewrite of our radio script."

"And?"

"Not too terrible," said Groucho.

Four

The next day started off chill and foggy. When I took off my hat after entering the small Bayside Diner at a few minutes after ten A.M., I noticed that it was damp with mist. The narrow restaurant appeared to be entirely empty, but then I heard a groaning noise coming from behind the counter.

Crossing the room, I went up on tiptoe to peer over.

Stretched out face down on the floor was a husky black man. Breathing heavily, he was doing pushups while counting to himself.

"Six . . . shit . . . seven . . . oh Jesus . . . eight . . . goddamn."

"Enery?" I inquired.

Enery McBride, who ran the Bayside most weekday mornings, let out a sigh and stretched out flat. "I have to get back in shape quick," he explained, not looking up. "That's because my career's taken a turn for the better."

"Which profession are we talking about?" I asked, settling onto a stool. "Fry cook or actor?"

Slowly he rolled over onto his back and then, groaning some more, he sat up. "Acting, Frank."

"Great. What?"

He scrambled up into a standing position. "I'm going to be playing royalty in a new movie that starts shooting over at Paragon come Monday."

"Royalty, huh?"

Enery nodded. "I'm signed to be the king of the cannibals in the latest TyGor the Jungle Boy flicker," he explained, grinning. "I think it's an impressive step upward from playing the porter in *Murder Express.*"

"Oh, without a doubt."

"If I keep on climbing at this rate, I'll be doing *Othello* for MGM in—what?—another year tops."

"Shouldn't even take that long." I glanced back at the door. "Anybody been by asking for me?"

"Not so far." Enery brushed dust off his white apron. "Coffee while you're waiting?"

"Might as well, sure."

"What do you think about Norma Shearer opposite me as Desdemona?"

"No, too old."

"Mae West?"

"Better."

He poured coffee into a tan mug and set it down in front of me.

I rested an elbow on the counter, asking, "You ever run into Peg McMorrow?"

Enery looked down, sighing again. "Yeah, poor kid," he answered. "It's funny, too, Frank. Because I heard she was going to be playing the white goddess in this latest TyGor epic."

"You sure?"

"Not a hundred percent, but the scuttlebutt was she was all set." He poured himself a mug of coffee. "So she shouldn't have been very unhappy, not like the papers said."

The door opened and I glanced over my shoulder.

George Tomley, a large wide man in his middle thirties came in. His blue suit already had a full day's worth of wrinkles and his polka dot tie was askew. He nodded at a rear booth without saying anything.

"Friend of yours?" asked Enery.

"A leftover from my reporter days, yeah." I gathered up my cup and headed for the booth.

"Morning," said Tomley in his raspy voice, settling into the seat.

Frowning, I sat down opposite him. "I don't notice any folder, George," I said. "Not even a memo."

"You're very perceptive." He rested both big hands flat on the tabletop. "That's a great asset for a crackerjack reporter."

"Or a crackerjack police detective like you, George," I said. "When I phoned you last night, you promised to sneak out the file on Peg McMorrow's death."

He hunched slightly, voice dropping lower. "The case is closed, Frank," he told me. "Shut tight. Over and done. On top of which, old buddy, the file turns out to be missing."

"C'mon, she only died yesterday," I said, eying him.

The plainclothes Bayside cop twisted his thick fingers together. "Seriously, Frank, this isn't anything you want to dig into any further. Okay?"

"Meaning what—some kind of coverup?"

He didn't say anything.

"What about getting a look at the autopsy report?"

After several silent seconds, Tomley replied, "That's not available."

I leaned forward. "Well, can you get me in to see her body?"

He shook his head. "Too late for that."

"What do you mean, George? They misplaced that, too?"

"She was cremated," he said, gesturing toward the foggy ocean outside. "And her ashes scattered over the Pacific."

"Who the hell's idea was that?"

"Hers."

"Oh, so? Where'd she request that—in a P.S. to her suicide note?"

Tomley coughed into one big hand. "I snuck over here to fill you in as best I can, Frank," he said. "Even if you were still a reporter with the *Times,* I'd advise you to forget about it. And, hell, as an *ex*-reporter—this sure isn't anything you want to fool with."

"Where's the pressure coming from, George?" I asked. "Are we talking about movie people, local hoods or—"

"We're not talking about anything." He rose up, lurched free of the booth. "This is just one more suicide. They happen all the time, especially around Hollywood." He leaned over, putting a hand on my shoulder. "It can be a very depressing town."

The big cop let go of me, nodded once and went walking out into the morning fog.

From behind the counter Enery called, "You want something to eat, Frank?"

Shaking my head, I got up. "Nope," I answered. "Turns out I don't have much of an appetite."

Five

At about the same time that I was getting nowhere with my most reliable contact on the Bayside police, Groucho, as he later told me, was slouching along La Cienega Boulevard in West Hollywood. He was wearing a tan checked sport coat, a lime green polo shirt and a pair of vaguely tweedy slacks. The cigar he was absently chewing on was unlit and his hands were thrust deep in his trouser pockets.

Someone made a gasping sound on his immediate left and he became aware that a plump woman in a flamboyantly flowered dress was walking along, sideways, next to him.

His eyebrows climbed. "Have you sprung a leak, madam?"

She gasped again. "You're," she began, pausing to inhale, "you're one of the Marx Brothers, aren't you?"

Groucho halted, scowled, removed the dead cigar from his lips and pointed at her with it. "No, my good woman, I'm actually *all* of the Ritz Brothers," he replied. "And let me tell you, it's a thankless task. Bad enough being Al and Jimmy, but being Harry as well takes all my spare time and you can't imagine how far behind I'm getting with my quilting." Reinstating the cigar, he resumed his slouching walk.

After taking another deep breath, the woman caught up with him and tugged a red-covered autograph album out of her black patent leather purse. "Well, I just know you're connected to the Marx Brothers in some way and so—"

"I'm connected with them in the worst way possible," he admitted, taking the album from between her pudgy fingers and opening it. "To Alice from John Gilbert," he read. "You've been at this nefarious pastime for a good many years, eh, Alice?"

"Since I was a girl."

"That is a long time." He accepted the stubby pencil she handed him and, after licking the tip, scribbled on a blank page. "Now, as pleasant as this interlude has been, Alice, I really must be going." He returned the book, kept the pencil and went loping off.

She brought the page up close to her eyes and read what Groucho had inscribed there. "Say," she called after him, "you signed this Hoot Gibson."

"You're extremely lucky," he returned over his shoulder. "Some days I don't even give a Hoot."

He turned onto the side street he'd been seeking, broke into a slow trot, went up the imitation marble steps and into the West Hollywood Athletic Club.

The tanned, blond young woman in the white shorts and white sweatshirt was shaking her head at Groucho. "You can't, really, go in there dressed like that, Mr. Marx."

"I know, it's awfully gauche of me," admitted Groucho, reaching again for the door of the Men's Steam Room. "But, alas, my only presentable tuxedo is away at the cleaner's. The cleaner himself, if you must know, is away down South in Dixie and as for his wife——"

"No, I mean, you've got your clothes on."

"We'll soon remedy that." Handing her his cigar butt, he started to slip out of his coat.

"You're supposed to undress in the locker room."

He narrowed his left eye and looked her up and down. "This is the darnedest proposition I've had in many a moon, my dear, but okay. Where's your locker room?"

"Not my locker room. The men's locker room, Mr. Marx."

"No, nope. Taking off my clothes in front of a bunch of fat men isn't my idea of fun," he informed her, putting his coat back on and taking the cigar. "Let's review the situation, shall we? You've already informed me that Abe Bockman, the famed talent agent and footpad, is within this very steam room getting parboiled even as we speak. Am I right thus far?"

"Yes, but——"

"I, on the other hand, am extremely eager to have a conversation with Abe."

"I heard your career was on the skids, but you still should be able to get a better agent than Abe Bockman."

"We can carry on this witty badinage all morning, child," he explained, "but eventually I'm going in there."

She gave a helpless sigh, turned around and went walking along the pale green hall toward her reception desk. "You're impossible," she said.

"My doctor assures me it's only a temporary condition," he told her through cupped hands.

He entered the steam room. Squinting into the thick white mist that started to engulf him, Groucho called out, "Abe?"

There was no response.

"Abe Bockman, I've got an important message from Sam Goldwyn."

"Over here," came a voice to his left. "Is it about the—"

"Welcome back from San Francisco." Groucho sat himself down on the bench next to the tall, lean agent.

"Well now, Groucho, I wasn't exactly up in Frisco, you know," Bockman said. He was wearing a yellow towel around his waist.

"I found that out, yes. And then I trailed you here. You see, mad silly creature that I am, I got the foolish notion you were trying to avoid me."

"I was trying to avoid everybody. Had to do with a little domestic problem. I decided to lie low for a couple days."

"What about your client—what about Peg?"

Bockman shook his head sadly. "A tragedy. But then show business is filled with— Ow!"

Groucho had taken hold of his upper arm, hard. "Abe, she didn't kill herself."

The agent pulled free of Groucho's grasp, went inching along the damp bench away from him. He stopped a few feet off, resting his palms on his sharp knees. "Maybe she didn't," he acknowledged.

Groucho, after using his pocket handkerchief to wipe his perspiring face, moved over beside him. "Then, what happened?"

"I don't know. I swear."

"She was a nice kid. Somebody killed her and—"

"Maybe she wasn't as nice as you think."

"Meaning what?"

"She changed quite a lot since you used to know her, Groucho. There are people she'd been hanging out with that—"

"What people? Who?"

Bockman glanced around at the thick mist. "Well, you know, I heard she was friendly with guys who work for Vince Salermo."

"The goniff who runs local gambling?"

"Right, him."

"Is Salermo involved in what happened to her?"

"I don't know and I wouldn't want to try to find out," the agent said quietly. "You don't annoy guys like Salermo, Groucho."

"I'm very good at annoying people," said Groucho evenly. "Especially when I'm already annoyed one hell of a lot myself."

Bockman said, "Hey, Groucho, listen. This whole town is built on rumors and gossip and out-and-out bullshit. Hell, probably Peg never even knew Salermo or any of his bunch."

Groucho wiped at his forehead again. "There was a girl Peg used to room with. Skinny blond tap-dancer who was in a couple of Busby Berkeley's Warner madrigals. She still around?"

"She called herself Sally St. Clair."

"That's the one. She was Peg's best friend," he said. "I'd like to talk to her."

"She got pregnant, went down to Mexico for a quick abortion, quit show business," recited the agent. "Last time I heard, which was maybe five, six months ago, she was working in the big Marcus Department Store in downtown L.A."

Off in a mist-shrouded corner of the steam room someone coughed loudly several times.

The agent got up abruptly, nearly losing his towel. "Well, I've been in the smokehouse long enough for one day," he announced. "Nice running into you again, Julius. Too bad about poor Peggy. Give my regards to your brothers, especially Zeppo. Even though he keeps trying to steal all my best clients."

Bockman readjusted his towel and walked off into the mist.

Groucho sat for a moment, chewing thoughtfully on the cigar and looking up toward where the ceiling ought to be.

Rising, he wiped his face once again. Then he walked carefully over to the corner.

The man who had coughed was large and hairy, wearing a red terrycloth robe. He seemingly hadn't sweated at all and his thick, dark hair was neatly combed. Groucho had never seen him before.

"You really should do something about that nagging cough," he suggested.

"And you, Mr. Marx, should get out of here before you wilt."

Nodding, Groucho headed for the doorway.

Six

The fog had nearly burned away when I got to the *Times* building down on West First in the heart of L.A.

I managed to get up to the floor I wanted without encountering anyone I'd worked with during my days on the police beat.

The small office I was visiting had DORA DAYTON, LOVELORN EDITOR lettered on the door in chipped gilt. I tapped three times on the frosted glass.

"Yeah?" came a sharp female voice.

"Me, May."

"C'mon in, Frank."

May Sankowitz was a small, slim woman up in her late forties. About five feet tall and a hundred pounds, her short-cropped hair had turned to red since last we'd met. She was seated behind an impressively cluttered wooden desk with her unshod feet up on it and her checkered skirt two or so inches above her knees.

A very tan, handsome and vacant young man, decked out in movie cowboy togs, was sitting on the edge of the desk with his back to her. He was concentrating on constructing a handmade cigarette with the tobacco from his sack of Bull Durham and a Zigzag paper. "Well, doggone it, May, I just can't not get the hang of rolling my own."

"Sometimes, Slim, I regret the advent of the talkies," she told him as she nudged him gently off the desk with the palms of both small hands. "Do your homework elsewhere, sweet."

"Dagnab it, we're going on location with *Vigilantes of Vacaville* day after tomorrow, hon," he complained as he went shuffling across the small office. "I just got to learn to roll my own with deftness and artistry by then." As he settled onto a folding chair, he touched the brim of his Stetson and grinned at me. "Howdy, pard."

"You'd never guess Slim was born in Youngstown, Ohio, would you, Frank?"

"Nope, I'd have thought Wisconsin."

"No need to fret over my accent, folks," said Slim, tearing a fresh cigarette paper out of the book. "I ain't got a speaking part in this here-now movie anyhow."

May swung her legs off the desk and sat up straight. She nodded at the cowboy actor. "You sure you don't want to go outside and lasso something, dear?"

"Nope."

She smiled at me across her Underwood typewriter. "Can I help it? I just happen to like tall, dumb men."

"Looks like you've hit paydirt this time." I settled into the chair that faced her desk.

"Shucks, I don't mind," Slim told me, "a little good-natured joshing."

"Fine." To May I said, "How's the lovelorn business?"

"You know what they say about the course of true love. Consequently, dear Dora is still pulling in sacks of forlorn mail daily—shit, hourly."

I asked, "You been able to dig up anything on the Peg McMorrow business for me?"

She rested one hand on a thin manila folder that sat atop a pile of other folders and sheets of copy. "Firstly, Frank, there isn't much in our morgue file on the girl," she said. "And, after some discreet inquiries amongst my colleagues, I haven't found out a whole hell of a lot about her recent suicide. Or should I say alleged suicide?"

"Probably alleged, May."

"I quizzed Al Levine, who covered her death for us," she continued. "He claims it was a routine suicide. See how blasé we get in this racket? Cute little kid bumps herself off and we call it routine."

"Al didn't notice anything unusual?"

"Listen, Frank, a Nazi submarine could've been parked on that starlet's front lawn and Al might not've noticed it. His version of what happens in a case like this is pretty much whatever the local cops tell him."

I nodded, having known Al Levine when I was with the paper. "What about pictures?"

"Well, there's a funny thing."

"How so?"

"The law didn't allow any picture taking."

"Who'd the *Times* send out?"

"Larry Shell. I asked him if he'd spotted anything." May touched at the left side of her forehead and then her temples.

"Larry did get a quick look at the body before they covered it up. He says the gal had bruises on her head and possible lacerations."

"From somebody hitting her?"

May shrugged. "Sure, possibly. Or maybe the kid fell out of her little coupe while she was still alive and banged her head on the garage floor."

"Maybe," I conceded.

Slim, who'd been intent on building a passable cigarette, looked up. "I can tell you something interesting about that poor little filly," he offered.

"You knew Peg?"

"Heck yes, in a casual way," replied the cowboy. "She had a pretty good part in *The Deputy Sheriff of Devil's Doorknob* over at Republic last summer and we chatted on a couple occasions. Nice kid she was, friendly."

Running her fingers through her bright red hair, May inquired, "Is that the sum and substance of your anecdote, dear?"

"Heck, honey, I ain't even got to the anecdote yet," he told her. "Hold your britches on and let me warm up to it, will you? Anyhow, about two weeks back I stopped in, pretty late at night, for a nightcap at the Blue Albatross out near Malibu."

"And?" persisted May.

"Wellsir, who should I spot hunkered down in a shadowy booth off in a far corner but Peg McMorrow," he continued in his patient drawling way. "Odd thing is—she was with Jack Gardella."

I frowned. "You sure, Slim? Gardella's the top troubleshooter over at Monarch Pictures. Important guy in Hollywood."

"Heck, I knew Gardella back when he was a strikebreaker in the late 1920s," Slim told me. "He was a mean and ornery son of a bitch then, if you'll pardon my lingo, and being chief goon at the biggest studio hereabouts and working for Eli Kurtzman sure ain't mellowed him none."

I nodded at May. "What would Peg be doing with him?"

"Maybe it was just a romantic fling."

"Sure, and maybe they were working on revisions of the Magna Carta, but I doubt that, too."

Leaning, she reached across the desk to touch my hand. "Look out for Gardella," she warned. "Tell you what—I'll see what I can find out about this angle. Lay off of him until you hear from me. You don't want to make him mad."

"I'm not sure about that," I said. "Could be I do."

She gave a negative shake of her head, gathered up the thin folder and handed it to me. "This is all the background stuff we have on Peg. Mostly it's the usual budding starlet crap, nightclubs and cheesecake. You can borrow it if you want."

"Thanks, May." I accepted the folder, tucking it under my arm and standing.

"What's the name of this new radio show you're working on?" she asked as I moved toward the door.

"Groucho Marx, Master Detective," I answered.

"Sounds funny."

"Yeah, funny," I said and left.

Seven

The fat man in the rumpled sharkskin suit dropped his big shopping bag as Groucho emerged from the elevator on the third floor of the vast Marcus Department Store.

"I know who you are," he exclaimed, clasping his plump hands together and producing a chuckling sort of sound inside himself someplace.

Groucho rushed up to him, taking long bent-knee steps, and clutched the fat man's upper left arm. "Then, praise the Lord, you're the very person I'm seeking," he confided. "I've been suffering from a nasty bout of amnesia for days now and, myself, have absolutely no idea who I am." He let go of the perplexed shopper's arm, took a step back and drew a fresh cigar out of his breast pocket. "You can't imagine, Mr. Hoffenstein, how serious a handicap amnesia can be to a—"

"My name isn't Hoffenstein," he put in. "I'm Edwin Silbersack."

Groucho gave a sad shake of his head. "Ah, then this is far worse than I supposed. Not only don't I remember who I am—gad, I don't even remember who *you* are."

"But you've never seen me before in your life."

"There now, Silbersack, no need to humor me. I'm sure we spent many happy childhood days together on the old plantation back—"

"I'm from Cleveland."

"Right you are, Cleveland is not noted for a high incidence of plantations." Groucho put the new cigar between his teeth. "Well, Edwin, this little strange interlude has cheered me up no end. And now, as it must to all men, I have to be up and doing." Taking hold of the fat man's right hand, he shook it vigorously.

"Well, nice to have met you, Mr. Marx."

Groucho had gone a few steps, but he halted, turned back and scowled. "What did you just call me?"

"Mr. Marx. You're Groucho Marx."

He dropped both hands to his sides and sighed profoundly. "Really? Darn," he said. "I was hoping I'd turn out to be Randolph Scott or, at the very least, Tom Mix. Somebody who'd look good on a horse. Because I got this horse as a present on my last birthday and the poor creature has just been standing around in the parlor, shifting from hoof to hoof, waiting for somebody to mount him." He sighed once more and then moved on.

"You can't smoke within the store, sir." A very slim and sleek floorwalker, wearing striped trousers, morning coat and white carnation, placed himself directly in Groucho's path.

"What gave you the idea, my good man, that I was intending to smoke?"

"That big fat cigar you've got dangling from—" The floorwalker recognized him then. "Oh, forgive me, Mr. Marx. I didn't immediately realize it was you. I mean, since you don't have a moustache in real life, I—"

"What's that you say?" Groucho brought up his free hand and patted at the clean-shaven skin immediately under his nose. "This is outrageous. I was in possession of a fine bushy moustache when I entered this shabby flea market and unless restitution is made I intend to sue. Well, possibly if prostitution is made, I'd settle for that."

The floorwalker giggled. "You're a very witty fellow, Mr. Marx."

"That's what they all keep telling me in my Girl Scout troop, yes," said Groucho. "Could you direct me to the vicinity of Sally St. Clair. They informed me down in the personnel office that she worked here on the third floor."

"That's right, Mr. Marx," he answered, giggling again. "I simply must tell you that the stateroom scene in *A Night at the Opera* is the funniest—"

"No, Chauncy, what you simply must tell me is how the heck to find Sally St. Clair."

"Yes, of course. I'm sorry."

"And well you should be, my lad."

"Miss St. Clair is in Kitchenware."

Shaking his head, Groucho addressed a skinny youth who'd paused to listen. "Wouldn't you know it? If only he'd said she was in Women's Underwear, I'm nearly certain I could've come up with some pithy rejoinder," he explained. "Or even if he'd told me she worked in Men's Hats, I might've been able to dredge up a cute saying. But Kitchenware just doesn't inspire."

The young man laughed. "I know who you are," he said shyly.

"Too late, sonny," Groucho informed him. "We've already done that routine. Now then, Chauncy, point me toward Sally."

"I'll do better than that, Mr. Marx, I'll personally escort you to her," he said. "Just walk this way."

Groucho followed, saying to the skinny young man, "I'm not even going to respond to an obvious setup like that."

Sally St. Clair was pale, blond, thin and weary-looking. She and Groucho were, with the permission of the floorwalker, sitting at a metal-topped patio table in the Outdoor Furniture section. Two imitation potted palms loomed up on Groucho's right.

"No," the thin girl was saying, "Peg would never commit suicide."

Resting his elbows on the tabletop, he said, "Okay, we agree about that. What I'm anxious to find out, Sally, is what really happened."

She shook her head. "I haven't, you know, seen much of Peg in the past few months, Mr. Marx. But . . ."

"But what?"

"Well, I did run into her, of all places, at the Farmers' Market a couple weeks ago," she said. "Peg looked swell and she was really excited."

"She tell you why?"

"Yes, she was going to sign a long-term movie contract."

"I've heard about that. Three years with Paragon."

"No, no, Mr. Marx." Sally shook her head again. "She had something in the works with Monarch."

"Monarch—you sure about that?"

"I am, yeah. I'd heard gossip about the Paragon deal and I asked her if she didn't mean Paragon. She laughed and said that Paragon was a second-rate outfit and that she was going to be working for the biggest studio in Hollywood," Sally explained. "Peg even told me that old man Kurtzman himself was going to make her the offer."

Groucho absently twisted the tip of an imitation palm frond around his forefinger. "Kurtzman was *going* to do this, huh? But he hadn't actually made the offer yet?"

"That's right, but she seemed awful smug about it. They were going to sign her and soon as they did, she'd see that Monarch found some work for me, too."

Letting go of the palm frond, Groucho said, "What about the fellows Peg was friendly with? Do you have any idea who she's been dating lately?"

"We didn't get around to talking about that when I ran into her." She leaned forward, lowering her voice. "Back when you were seeing her, you know, there were other guys, too."

"Yeah, I knew Peg wasn't especially faithful," he acknowledged. "That's only fair really, since Peg wasn't the only young lady—and that's not even including my wife—that I was wooing at the time."

"You know who Shel Leverson is, don't you?"

"A hoodlum," answered Groucho. "He one of Peg's beaus?"

"She never told me that, but somebody else did about six months ago."

"Leverson is the right-hand man—or maybe it's the left-hand man—of Vince Salermo, king of the gamblers," said Groucho. "Not nice guys."

"I think she was pretty much a decent girl," Sally said. "But, you know, she got a kick out of taking risks. It was fun to her to date a punk like Leverson or to go down to Tijuana and gamble or . . ." Her voice trailed off. "Well, really, that's about all I know."

"If you remember anything else, give me a call, huh?"

Her laugh was brief and dry. "C'mon, Mr. Marx, your servants wouldn't even put me through to you."

He gave her a phone number. "I'm the only one who answers that particular phone, Sally." He started to get up.

She caught at his coat sleeve. "Listen, I'm not much of a dancer anymore," she told him. "But I think I can still do bit parts. If you run into anybody who—"

"I'll have Zeppo give you a call."

"An agent like him will never phone me."

Groucho sat down again and took her hand. "He'll phone you," he promised her. "You have my word."

She pulled her hand free. "We'll see," she said.

Eight

I drove by Peg McMorrow's cottage on my way to pick up Jane late that afternoon.

All was quiet and it looked just like any other inexpensive beach house. The garage was shut tight.

On my car radio Knox Manning was doing the news and I turned him off in the middle of something about Great Britain's latest attempt to appease Hitler so that I could talk to myself uninterrupted.

"I wonder if her car's in the garage."

If it was still there, we ought to take a look at it.

"Larry Shell's pretty reliable. If he says Peg had head injuries, then she did."

I reminded myself that it would also be a good idea to talk directly with the *Los Angeles Times* photographer to make sure he could confirm what May Sankowitz had passed along to me.

"Groucho's right about this. Peg wasn't a suicide."

I turned onto Palm Lane, which had only one palm tree, and a woebegone one at that, on its entire seven-block length.

The final block dead-ended against a scrubby hillside. I parked in front of 1343. Rod Tommerlin had been doing a very successful comic strip for the past three years and his house was large and strived to be impressive. It had a lot of glass and redwood in its makeup and was obviously designed by someone who idolized Frank Lloyd Wright without quite grasping his basic principles.

As I went striding up the flagstone pathway that curved across the vast green lawn, I heard a crashing sound from inside the house.

A man shouted "God damn!" and I sprinted for the door.

The chimes played "She'll Be Comin' 'Round the Mountain," no doubt an allusion to Hillbilly Willie.

Jane answered the door, her face slightly flushed and a strand of her auburn hair down across her forehead. "Oh hi," she said, smiling and inhaling at the same time. "You're a few minutes early."

I scrutinized her. She was wearing a short-sleeved white blouse and a tan skirt and there were a few black inky smudges on her bare left arm. "You okay?" I inquired.

"Fine," she assured me. "Fine and dandy, in fact."

I made a skeptical noise. "What fell over?"

"Beg pardon?" Jane took a few steps back, beckoning me to cross the threshold into the high-ceilinged foyer of the cartoonist's house.

"I heard something crash and then somebody yowled."

"Oh, that." She led me into a very large and very bright glassy living room.

"Details?" I suggested.

"Rod fell down."

"He do that often?"

She brushed her hair from her forehead. "He just tripped over some research material."

I nodded. "Okay, yes. I've heard that's a common household accident."

"Hey, everything is okay," she said. "So would you like to drive me home or would you prefer to loiter around here and make snide remarks?"

"Don't I get to meet your boss?"

"Not today, Frank. Rod's trying to finish up a Sunday page so he can get it off on the last airmail plane to New York City." From the arm of a low white sofa she picked up a cardigan sweater. "Let's go, huh?"

We didn't do much in the way of conversing until she was in the car and heading for her place.

"How was your day?" Jane asked, watching the bright late afternoon outside.

"Did that jerk make a pass at you?"

"Rod's not a jerk," she answered, a bit primly I thought. "And no, he did not."

"If he did, I think I'd better—"

"Trust me, please, nothing happened. And if something had, I know how to take care of myself."

"All right, okay," I said. "What can I do to appease you?"

She smiled. "By the way, I have to work tonight."

"Back there?"

"No, dimwit. In the privacy of my own home, doing some *Hillbilly Willie* promotion drawings that are overdue," she explained. "If you're free after, say, ten tonight, you can drop by and we can have coffee and hold hands." She turned in the seat, looking at me. "That is, after you've searched all the closets and peeked under my bed for rival suitors."

"You are obviously not accustomed to keeping company with a chivalrous westerner, ma'am," I observed, slowing down to park in front of her cottage. The little shingled house wasn't that different from Peg McMorrow's and, for a moment, that made me feel very uneasy.

Jane said, "I guess you're right. Excuse it, please."

"Tonight will work out," I said, sliding out of the car. I trotted around and opened her door for her. "Because I promised to go over to Groucho's in about an hour so we can compare notes on our day's activities."

"Did *your* day's activities include working on the script for the radio show?"

"That only needs a few minor changes."

"Uh-huh." We sat side by side on the top step of her porch. "You think there really is something to his suspicions about her death?"

"I do, yeah."

We had a fine view of the Pacific Ocean. It was only a few hundred feet downhill and gradually, as we talked and I filled her in on what I'd been up to, the day began to wane and the water turned first a paler blue and then started to darken.

When I'd finished, Jane tightened her grip on my hand. "You're going to get hurt," she warned. "Really, you and Groucho are poking into something that—"

"I know, we might be going up against some fairly dangerous hoods or some very powerful moguls. Or both," I admitted. "Thing is, if Peg was murdered, hell, something has to be done about it."

"Agreed, but not necessarily by an aging comedian and a chivalrous radio writer. This is what the police are supposed to take care of."

"The Bayside cops are part of the coverup, way it looks."

"How about the state police or the mayor or the governor or—"

"California is noted for its mild climate, but not especially for its clean government," I said. "Hell, I wouldn't know, at least at this point, who we can trust."

"Even so, Frank, you babes in the woods need some kind of professional help."

Leaning, I kissed her on the cheek. Then I reluctantly stood up. "I'll convey all this to Groucho," I said. "And I'll see you again around ten."

"Be sure you don't get yourself killed before then."

"I shall," I promised, "make every effort to remain extant."

Twilight was spreading slowly through Beverly Hills as I swung off Santa Monica Boulevard onto North Hillcrest Road. Groucho was residing in a sprawling tile-roofed Monterey-style house at number 710. It was a big whitewashed place that he'd described to me as trying to look like "something put up by a gaggle of tipsy Spanish missionaries."

Parking in the white gravel drive, I went up to the front door and reached for the brass knocker.

Before I could touch it, the oaken door swung open inward. "Good evening, sir."

Groucho, wearing a tatty flannel bathrobe dotted with faded orange sunbursts on a field of washed-out turquoise, was standing there looking vaguely British.

"Evening, I—"

"I'm Chives, sir, Mr. Marx's loyal major-domo," Groucho explained in a vaguely British accent. "I used to be his major homo but the bobbies put a stop to that. The master is upstairs dallying with the downstairs maid—or possibly he's downstairs dallying with the upstairs maid." He shrugged. "Be that as it may, I've been instructed to invite you in and inform you that the master will be with you presently. Or if you can't wait, I can bewitch you on the spot. And you even get to select the spot from twenty-three convenient locations."

"Very impressive, Mr. Marx," I told him, stepping into the large hallway. "But we've already cast Eric Blore in the part."

"I feared as much," said Groucho, signaling me to follow him along the hallway. "That Screen Pansies Guild has all the good butler and valet parts sewn up tight. And if you're going to get sewn up, say, you may as well be tight." He loped into a big white kitchen, readjusted his robe and seated himself at a round table. "You arrived early, Rollo."

"Everybody's been telling me that."

"Best take it to heart." There was a pastrami sandwich on a white plate in front of him. "You'd think that a society that had invented the wheel, perfected roller-skates and found a cure for hay fever would be able to produce a passable New York-style pastrami on rye."

"They haven't found a cure for hay fever."

"Ah, then that explains this sandwich." He pushed the plate a few inches away from him. "My family—whom I like to refer to as One Man's Family because it's much catchier than, oh, say, the Kate Smith Show—is not at home," he informed me, gesturing vaguely at the kitchen walls. "Arthur, my only-begotten son, is off playing tennis somewhere. Tennis is his passion, as it was mine until I discovered jellybeans. My sweet little daughter, Miriam, is attending a pajama party with a coven of equally giggly girls. And my wife . . . well, she's out and about. So what do you think, Mr. Anthony? Can this marriage be saved? And if it can, what precisely would you save it in? A bucket, a cardboard box or . . . But I seem to have strayed from the point."

"Oh, so? I hadn't noticed."

Groucho poked the top of his sandwich and narrowed his left eye. "You come perilously close, Merriwell, to being a wiseass."

"I only need five more credits and I get my certificate." I sat across from him. "Shall we talk about Peg McMorrow now?"

Groucho sighed what sounded like a genuinely sad sigh. "Yeah, let's move on to that." He suddenly jumped up, motioning me to stay put. "Sit, Rollo, I want to get something to show you."

I sat and in just under five minutes he was back with a somewhat wrinkled manila envelope. "I keep these hidden," Groucho explained, returning to his chair. "Souvenirs of the lost past are, as Marcel Proust reminds us, hunky dory. However, there's no need to leave them lying around where jealous mates can find them."

"These are pictures of Peg?"

Nodding, Groucho reached into the envelope and drew out three snapshots and two glossy portraits. He spread them out, facing me, on the tabletop. "The snaps were taken down in a little out-of-the-way Mexican resort town. The studio shots are what Abe Bockman uses—used—to peddle her flesh around town."

The girl in the snapshots was very pretty, slim and dark-haired. She looked relaxed and happy, both feistiness and vulnerability showing in her high-cheekboned face. Wearing a two-piece sunsuit, she was leaning against a stretch of adobe wall in two of the pictures. Groucho was in the third with her, one arm around her, grinning, looking happy, too.

The Peg in the formal portraits was somebody else, guarded and calculating.

"Being with you improved her," I told him, looking up.

"Mostly I knew the Peggy in those snaps," he told me. "A nice kid with a sense of humor and, yes, very affectionate. But that other Peg . . ." He turned both of the portraits face down, shaking his head. "You understand, Frank, that I don't mind helping a beginning actress get a start in this lousy business. Peg, though, got to be too obvious about it, about using me. That was the reason I quit seeing her." He gathered all the pictures up and put them away in the manila envelope again.

"Which Peg prompted someone to kill her?"

He said, "Let's talk about what we came up with today. Then we can draw up an agenda for tonight's activities."

"Tonight's activities?"

"Of course, Philo, the game's afoot."

"It better not be afoot after ten," I mentioned. "I got a date with Jane."

Nine

The gaunt undertaker shot his starched white cuffs, leaned forward and rested both sharp elbows on his desk. "It's time, Mr. Marx," he suggested in his deep, slightly droning voice, "that you started thinking about your own eternal rest. We here at the Everlasting Repose Chapel and Mortuary have several satisfying plans that will assure those who love you that once you've shuffled off this—"

"Actually, Whitman," Groucho informed the pale, thin man from our side of the desk, "you'd get a bigger, and a better behaved and dressed, crowd if you concentrated on those who loathe me. However, I'm not ready for eternal rest." He extracted a fresh cigar from the breast pocket of his avocado-colored sport coat. "Though maybe a series of short naps might not be bad."

Ethan Whitman allowed himself to frown. "Perhaps you'd better explain exactly why you're paying me this rather late visit, then."

"I've been, quite pithily I thought, working up to that, Whitman."

I glanced again at my wristwatch. Nine o'clock was drawing nearer. "This has to do with Peg McMorrow's body," I put in.

Whitman's frown deepened and he turned to look directly at me. "Peg McMorrow?" He gave a brisk, negative shake of his pale head. "No, I don't believe we've processed anyone of that name through the chapel."

"Ah, but you have, Whitman," Groucho corrected. "My associate here, a shrewd lad despite his strong resemblance to a rustic bumpkin, found that out." He patted my shoulder. "He used to be a crime reporter."

"Because Bayside doesn't have its own," I added, "I know that two of our prominent funeral parlors take turns acting as the morgue. Peg McMorrow's body was brought here for its autopsy."

After sitting up straighter in his chair and shooting his cuffs again, Whitman told us, "I'm afraid you've been misinformed, gentlemen."

"Banana oil," observed Groucho, fishing a book of matches from the Trocadero out of his side pocket. "The autopsy *was* performed here and you later shipped her body off to be cremated. What we want you to tell us is"—he held up his left hand, fingers spread wide, and started to tick them off— "One. Who ordered that cremation? Two. What were the results of—"

"I'm sure that you probably are as astute as Mr. Marx claims," the undertaker said to me, his chill look containing a trace of pity for my incurable stupidity. "Be that as it may, I can assure you that I'm unfamiliar with Peg McMorrow and that she was never in my establishment." He scowled in Groucho's direction. "I recall now reading an account of the poor child's unfortunate suicide in the newspaper yesterday, but that is absolutely all I know about her."

Groucho lit the cigar and then took a deep drag on it. "See here, Whitman, I resent—" Suddenly smoke came spilling out of his nose. Leaning far over, he began to cough violently.

When I reached over to thwack him on the back, he waved me away and continued to cough.

Groucho went lurching out of his chair and tottered over to the door. Still coughing and spilling out cigar smoke, he dived into the hall. "Glass of water," he called as he went loping off.

The undertaker rested his arms again on his desk. "I'll confide something in you."

"About Peg McMorrow?"

"No, no, don't be ridiculous, Mr. Denby," said Whitman, his frown deepening. "I was merely going to mention that I've never found Mr. Marx particularly funny in the movies." He shook his head. "My idea of a truly amusing motion picture comedian is Buster Keaton—as well as Harry Langdon and Harold Lloyd."

"None of them makes many films these days."

"Yes, and it's a pity. I can recall that—" He stood up, glancing toward the doorway. "Feeling better, Mr. Marx?"

"Fit as a fiddle," Groucho assured the undertaker, easing over toward the desk. "In fact, fit as a tuba, which is bigger and brassier and accepted in all the best places. Shall we go forth into the night, Rollo?"

I rose up out of my chair, eying him. "If your spasms have subsided, sure."

"I am entirely spasm-free." When I was standing between him and Whitman, Groucho gave me a quick wink. "Except for having coughed up several feet of intestine, I am as good as new." He leaned around me, giving the funeral director a lazy salute. "Thank you for your time and courtesy, Whitman. The next dead man I run into, I'll surely recommend you to him."

"Good evening, Mr. Marx," Whitman said. "I do hope you'll be able to find work now that your movie career is at an end."

Out in the shadowy, floral-scented and thickly-carpeted corridor, Groucho leaned close and whispered, "Have no fear, Sergeant Heath, I've—" He stopped talking and frowned down the hall. "Ixnay, it's an umpchay."

Standing in a doorway at the far end of the hall was a tall young man of about twenty. He had a broom in one hand and was wearing a pair of faded overalls. He was watching Groucho with what can only be described as a sappy grin on his face.

"Your admirers are everywhere," I suggested as he took hold of my arm and tugged me in the direction of the front door.

"Nonsense, an admirer of an artist of my caliber would never seek employment as a janitor in a run-down abattoir like this," Groucho pointed out. "I also might've said that an admirer of mine wouldn't be caught dead in a place like this. But that's probably too obvious, huh?"

"Too obvious, yeah."

When we were out in the faintly misty night and moving away from the sprawling thatch-roofed building, Groucho said, "We'll pop back and poke around after that putz Whitman departs for the day. I hope to Jehovah he doesn't spend his nights inside there, sleeping in one of his coffins."

"How are we getting back inside?"

"I took the opportunity, while out pretending to recuperate from my bronchial seizure, of slipping a matchbook between the door and the doorjamb of the side entryway to Repose Room Three," he explained as we neared my yellow coupe. "We'll head over to Peg's cottage now and after we've searched there, we'll sneak back inside this morbid wickiup and—"

"You expect to accomplish all this in under an hour, do you?" I inquired as I slid in behind the wheel. "Because, as I've probably mentioned before—"

"As you've *probably* mentioned, Nurse Jane? You've been babbling about your upcoming assignation with this bit of fluff ever since we ventured forth on—"

"The point is, Groucho, I really would like to wind things up tonight by ten."

"Keep in mind, young man," stated Groucho as the car pulled away from the curb, "that the weariest river runs not smoothly but too well and that many a Maxie Rosenbloom is born to blush in the desert air."

"All too true," I conceded, aiming my car toward Peg Mc-Morrow's cottage. "But what in the hell does it have to do with the situation at hand?"

"Not a blessed thing," he admitted. "I'm just attempting to keep you distracted until we do what has to be done." He paused, looking out into the thickening mist. "This is, no kidding, important to me."

After a moment I said, "I know, yeah. Okay, I can be a little late getting to Jane's."

"That's the spirit. You're exactly the kind of man we're looking for in the Salvation Army," said Groucho, smiling. "Come around to headquarters in the morning and we'll issue you your tambourine."

Ten

Out in the bay, somewhere unseen, foghorns were calling.

Next to me on the shadowy back porch of Peg McMorrow's cottage Groucho quietly remarked, "What Boy Scout troop did you acquire this trick from?"

Ignoring him, I concentrated on picking the back door lock.

"I suppose they couldn't openly award you a merit badge in housebreaking," he continued, teeth clamped on his dead cigar. "Though, lord knows, it's a lot more valuable knack than being able to roast weenies over a sooty campfire."

The lock finally produced a gratifying click. I nodded and very carefully turned the knob. The door creaked faintly as I urged it slowly open.

We crossed the dark threshold into the kitchen and I shut the door. The small room smelled thickly of stale coffee and cigarettes.

"I have the impression I just stepped in a patch of Jell-O." Groucho clicked on the small flashlight he'd brought along and illuminated the floor.

What he'd trod on was a sponge.

It would've been difficult not to have stepped on something. All the drawers had been yanked out and their contents dumped on the yellow linoleum flooring. The cabinets, too, had been ransacked and even a wicker basket that held movie magazines had been upended and searched.

The beam of Groucho's light brushed across smiling images of Myrna Loy, Joan Crawford and Eleanor Powell. "Did I ever tell you what transpired between Crawford and me in a cramped phone booth south of the border?"

"Nope."

"Just as well." He played the light around the room. "You know more than I do about how the local bobbies operate. Would you say this was their work?"

I shook my head. "They're somewhat less obvious than this."

He leaned his backside against the edge of the small white-painted kitchen table. "Which means somebody's been poking here."

"Yeah. Most likely hunting for something small *and* flat."

"What makes you say that, Rollo?"

"Well, they dumped out the silverware drawer," I pointed out. "That indicates, unless they were just out to make an ungodly mess, they were hunting a relatively small object. But they also tore that scenic calendar off the wall and flipped through it. Which suggests something flat that could be hidden behind a page."

"Letters?" suggested Groucho. "Pictures? Bonds? Money? Legal documents?"

"Any of those, yeah."

"I doubt Peg kept much in the way of cash, bonds or stock

certificates around her digs." Groucho straightened up. "Before we inspect the rest of her place, I want to take a gander in the garage." He, flashlight dangling at his side, went loping into the hallway.

"Holy mackerel!" I heard him remark from up front in the living room.

I caught up with him and saw what he'd seen.

The living room had been very thoroughly searched. Everything that had been on the walls—pictures, photos—was on the floor. Apparently impatient when the glass doors on the small bookcase wouldn't immediately open, the searchers had smashed them and dragged all the books and bric-a-brac out. Every sofa cushion and chair cushion had been removed and slashed open. Feathers, cotton and some kind of crunchy sawdust were strewn all across the faded carpet.

"Bastards," muttered Groucho, sitting on the arm of the devastated sofa and shining the flashlight at the debris.

"Somebody wanted something she had, something important to them," I said. "I wonder if that's why they killed her—and if they found what they were hunting for."

"Goddamned cops." Groucho, angry, stood up. "They come in here on their big flat feet, they see this godawful mess—and what? Do they think Peg tossed her own house before stepping into the damn garage to kill herself?"

"They overlooked the fact she was murdered," I reminded him. "They could sure as hell overlook this."

I could see his face in the glow from the flashlight in his hand. His expression shifted suddenly from anger to perplexity. "What is it?" I asked.

He snapped his fingers. "What did I show you up at my palatial mansion?"

"A second-rate pastrami sandwich?"

"Besides that."

"Pictures of you and Peg."

"Exactly." Crouching, he started a more thorough inspection of the stuff that was scattered about the room. "Peg loved to snap pictures, always had a couple of cheap cameras around. She used to carry a Kodak Brownie with her all the time. But I don't see a camera anywhere."

"Where'd she keep her pictures?" I was moving in his wake, checking over the spill on the floor.

Groucho halted, frowning back at me. "You're right, Rollo. We haven't seen hide nor hair of a camera and there's no sign of any of the little fat photo albums she had," he said. "They might be in her bedroom, but I have a hunch we won't find 'em there either."

That turned out to be true. The bedroom, which was thick with the scent of a floral perfume that reminded me of the funeral parlor, had been thoroughly searched, as had the tiny room where Peg had kept the boxes she never got around to unpacking. We found no cameras and no collections of photographs.

Groucho, however, did come across a couple of interesting items. One was a meal check from the True Blue Cafeteria over in Hollywood.

"This dump is right around the corner from the Young Actresses' Club where Peg used to live when she first hit town."

"And?"

"You're not being observant," he mentioned, using the light as a pointer. "This happens to be dated just last week."

"You mean you're curious as to why Peg'd be having a seventy-five-cent dinner in a place where she probably hadn't eaten in years?"

"That's what strikes me as odd, uh-huh." He folded the yellow slip of paper and deposited it in a side pocket of his coat.

The meal check he found beside the bed. Next to the toppled dressing table bench he spotted a receipt from the Mermaid Water Taxi Service of Santa Monica. Holding it up, he said, "This is the outfit that runs suckers out to the *Encantada.* That's the gambling ship moored off Pacific Palisades and—"

"I know. I was over there once or twice when I was working for the *Times.*"

"My dearly beloved brother Chico has been ferried over to that barge far too many times to count. Where he ever got the notion he could beat the system and . . ." Groucho sighed, shook his head and dropped the receipt into the same pocket with the meal check. "Peg was over there just three nights ago."

"Vince Salermo operates the *Encantada,*" I said. "According to what you found out from her onetime roommate, Peg was seeing Shel Leverson, one of Salermo's goons."

"Could be Leverson, and maybe Salermo, were among the last people Peg ever saw."

"Be interesting to find out if she had a reason besides gambling when she went to that ship."

"We'll do that," promised Groucho.

* * *

The garage, when we finally got around to it, was disappointing.

Well, not exactly disappointing. It simply didn't offer any overt information about the cause of Peg McMorrow's death.

Unlike the cottage, the garage was neat and clean. It was also totally empty.

The car the young actress had died in wasn't there. And not a box or a tool or even a scrap of paper remained. In addition, the gray cement floor had been very recently scrubbed and scoured.

"The absence of anything," announced Groucho after we'd taken it all in, "is the biggest clue we've come across so far."

"Possibly, but difficult to bring into court."

"Even so, it's obvious that someone has been working damned hard to remove all traces of what the hell really happened here," he said. "Nobody would go to that trouble to cover up a suicide."

"The thing is, Groucho, this couldn't have been done without the Bayside police knowing about it."

"We already agreed that the local gendarmes are goniffs." He handed me the flashlight, inserted a fresh cigar into his mouth and began, with hands locked behind his back and shoulders hunched, to pace the spotless garage. "Can we, do you think, find her car and get a look at it?"

"Probably not," I answered. "I'd bet that it's either at the bottom of a lake by now or in the process of being dismantled at some remote junkyard."

"I suppose we— Hold it." He dropped to his knees suddenly. "Shine the light here."

I did.

He was poking his finger at a small, faint brownish spot on the concrete. "That's a bloodstain. That proves that Peg was—"

"Nope, all it proves is that she shed a drop of blood in here in the recent past."

"You know damn well they killed her." He stood up, hands on hips, glaring at me. "So why are you standing there like a schmuck and pretending that—"

"Hey." I took hold of his arm. "You know Peg was murdered. I know she was murdered. Hell, the police know it, too," I said evenly. "But, for reasons we don't yet know, it was covered up."

"Unhand me and—"

"Listen now. Losing our tempers and yelling at each other isn't going to help," I told him. "If we're going to find out who killed her and—more importantly—bring them to justice, then, c'mon, Groucho, we have to keep calm and cool and calculating. Okay?"

Groucho chewed on the end of his unlit cigar for a few silent seconds. "No one has dared address me in that tone before, suh," he said finally. "But, damme, lad, I admire your spunk and when I order you keelhauled, why, sirrah, I'm going to instruct Midshipman Easy to use only little itsy-bitsy barnacles." He moved back from me, turning away.

"I think we've uncovered about all we can here," I told him, moving toward the door into the darkened cottage. "We don't want to linger."

Groucho was quiet as we made our way back through the house.

Very carefully I eased the rear door open. The mist was thicker and the foghorns were still calling.

I stepped out into the night first, followed by Groucho.

I'd only taken three steps across the damp lawn when somebody tried to kill us.

Eleven

I heard the loud chuffing sound, heard the slug go thunking into the wood of the door just behind me, then realized I was being shot at.

"Down," I warned, diving for the ground.

Groucho was already on the lawn, muttering, rolling in the direction of a low, sparse hedge.

Another shot came, this one digging a rut only a few inches from his head.

"Gentlemen, this is hardly sporting," he observed, scurrying toward a break in the hedge.

The third slug dug up grass uncomfortably close to my left ribs.

Down the block a dog had started barking vigorously.

Then a woman opened a window and started yelling. "What the hell is going on? Stop that!"

There were no more shots. Then a car engine came to life.

Because of the fog I never got a look at whoever it was that was shooting at us. And I didn't see the car that went roaring away now.

"Can you beat that?" Groucho sat up. "That old biddy told them to stop and they did." He, groaning once, wobbled to his feet. "Why didn't I think of that?"

"You okay?"

"A shade moist from frolicking in the topsoil, but otherwise hunky-dory. And you?"

"I'm all right," I told him. "What say we get the hell out of the vicinity, before someone summons the law."

"Or unleashes that hound."

We headed for the next block, where we'd left my car under a pepper tree.

Just as I started the car, I became aware of distant sirens. "Cops," I observed, pulling away from the curb.

"Did you get a look at the bozos who mistook us for fish in a barrel?"

"Nope. Did you?"

"Chiefly I was viewing lawn from an entirely new and fresh perspective," he admitted. "Too damn foggy to see much anyway. How many do you figure there were?"

"Probably just one doing the shooting."

"Yes, I suppose for these small-change assassinations that's sufficient." He leaned back in his seat, rubbing at a grass stain on his knee.

I drove as rapidly but unobtrusively as I could away from there.

The Everlasting Repose Chapel and Mortuary sat dark and silent in the night fog. Even the sedate neon sign mounted above the slanting thatch roof had been turned off. The parking lot was empty except for a lone gray hearse spotted with mist.

We'd parked across the street, as far from a street lamp as possible, and directly under a forlorn palm tree. Down at the opposite end of the block was a gas station and it, too, was dark and deserted. There was a phone booth planted next to the rest rooms and, while Groucho watched the funeral home to make absolutely certain nobody was still in there, I slipped quietly out of the driver's seat and jogged down to the phone.

The overhead light refused to go on when I shut the door. Since the booth gave strong evidence that someone had recently been sick therein, I decided it was better to leave the door open and let in the night air and fog.

Jane answered on the second ring. "Okay, all right. But don't call me anymore tonight," she began in an angry voice.

"Do I win any sort of prize if I guess what in the hell you are talking about?" I inquired.

"Oh, sorry. I thought you were somebody else."

"Glad I'm not. Who was that meant for?"

"Never mind," she said, anger gone. "Although I'm somewhat miffed at you. It is, by my reckoning, already ten-thirty."

"I know, that's why I'm phoning."

"Are you planning to arrive here at all tonight?"

"Yes, if you don't mind my not getting there till around eleven."

"Has something gone wrong?"

"Well, I could play for sympathy and tell you I got shot at, but I'd rather—"

"You got shot? Jesus."

"No, shot *at.*"

"That's bad enough. What—"

"I'll fill you in when I get there. They shot at Groucho, too, but we both escaped injury."

"Who did it?"

"You couldn't spot anybody in the fog. We were coming out of Peg McMorrow's cottage when—"

"I've been trying to convince you, Frank, that both of you are messing in something very dangerous."

"We'll thrash this out later. If you're going to be up that late."

"Who can sleep when the man she may well love is out getting shot at?"

"That's very flattering. Is—"

"Go finish up whatever foolhardy thing it is you're doing. Then hurry over. Goodbye." She hung up.

I went hurrying back to the coupe.

Groucho hopped free of the car. "Appropriately enough," he announced, "there's not a sign of life yonder."

"Let's sneak in and look around, then."

No one had spotted the matchbook Groucho'd stuck in the side door earlier to keep it from shutting completely and locking. The heavy door made a faint metallic groan as we, carefully and slowly, shoved it open.

Repose Room 3 was untenanted and smelled, as did just about everything in the mortuary, of dying flowers.

Tugging out his flashlight, Groucho clicked it on. "When I was prowling this mausoleum earlier in the evening, I noticed a room full of filing cabinets just across from the bathrooms," he said. "They may have a folder on Peg stashed away in there someplace."

We moved, more or less on tiptoe, out into the long, dark corridor.

"Should somebody succeed in knocking me off later in the evening," whispered Groucho, "please plead with my next of kin not to ship me to this particular establishment to be processed by Ethan Whitman and his gang of ghouls. Ethan Whitman and his All Ghoul Orchestra? Is that up to my usual standard?"

"I didn't know you had standards."

"I see. We'll both count to a hundred and then pretend I never said it."

"Best course of action, yes."

Groucho led me to an office door, nodded at it. "In here, Sherlocko," he invited and opened the door wide.

In the glow from his light I could make out that three walls of the room held rows of green metal filing cabinets. The fourth wall was taken up with a large chart illustrating the wide variety of caskets the chapel was prepared to lay you away in.

"That number twenty-six matches your eyes, Rollo." He swung the flashlight beam up to touch the chart. "And that fetching raccoon tail you use to festoon your jalopy would look absolutely stunning hung from one of those gilded handles."

Moving over closer to the filing cabinets, I started checking the tags on the drawers. "This looks like *M–N* here, Groucho," I said, tugging out a drawer as he came over beside me.

"There it is," he said, elated, shining the beam on the folder I was lifting out of the pack.

I hadn't expected it to be there, but it was. A manila folder with *McMorrow, Peg* typed neatly on its bright new label. "So they didn't destroy everything."

"Open it already."

"Damn." There was only a single half sheet of paper inside. No autopsy report, nothing else.

"Still, this is something." Holding the light with his chin, Groucho took the slip of pale blue paper in both hands.

It was a receipt, typed on Eternal Repose Chapel and Mortuary letterhead and acknowledging the receipt of $250. The fee was to pay for transporting Peg McMorrow's body to the Undying Flame Crematorium in Altadena and arranging for it to be cremated. The bill had been paid by Justin LaSalle.

"How the devil does that pansy figure in this?"

"Used to be in pictures, didn't he?"

"Briefly, a few years back. Then somebody decided to tote up all the high school boys he'd buggered," explained Groucho. "Well, it turned out LaSalle had gone way over the quota, even the special quota established for Hollywood. So he was tossed out on his keister by Paramount and they replaced him with three interchangeable new gigolos. LaSalle went into the interior decorating trade and, when last I heard, was flourishing."

"Did he know Peg?"

Groucho tucked the receipt away in another pocket and took the flashlight from under his chin. "She never mentioned him, but that doesn't prove a damn thing," he said.

"We'd better add LaSalle to the list of people we—"

All the lights in the room suddenly blossomed into life. From the doorway behind us a soft voice said, "Good evening, Mr. Marx."

Twelve

Groucho said, "This is the first time I've ever signed an autograph in a morgue."

"I really appreciate this, Mr. Marx," said the lanky young man in the overalls.

"What was your name again?" asked Groucho, taking the proffered autograph book and fountain pen.

"Tristan Fahrland, sir."

" 'To Tristan,' " muttered Groucho as he scribbled on a page. " 'With the undying respect of' "—he paused, glancing up at the ceiling—" 'Groucho Marx.' " Capping the pen, he handed it and the book back to the young mortuary janitor.

Tristan scanned the inscription, smiled. "Thank you very much, Mr. Marx," he said, tucking the book away in the bib pocket. "I'm glad I hung around here in the dark and waited."

"And I'm glad you didn't turn out to be a gunman."

"How exactly," I asked, "did you figure out we'd be returning?"

The young man answered, "Oh, well, I happened to overhear you talking to Mr. Whitman. So I knew you were interested in the actress who died."

"And?"

"Then I happened to see Mr. Marx job the side door here," Tristan continued. "That got me to thinking, you know, that you'd probably be trying to sneak back in here to find out more about her. Because old Whitman sure as hell wasn't going to tell you much."

"Your loyalty to Whitman is not pronounced," observed Groucho.

"He's a jerk," said Tristan. "And he lied to you. I've seen just about all your movies, Mr. Marx, and I like them a lot, except for the parts where Harpo plays the harp. That's really not very funny."

"Try to convince Harpo of that." Groucho raised his eyebrows and rolled his eyes.

"By the way, sir, you look a lot funnier with a moustache."

"I know," said Groucho. "But they made me stop wearing it in public because too many people were falling down in fits of laughter. While others were falling down in gutters. At the moment my moustache is being kept in a bird cage at a nonspecific location in Beverly Hills, and as it rocks on its perch it sadly sings, 'I'm only a beard in a gilded cage, a—' "

"What," I cut in, "do you know about Peg McMorrow, Tristan?"

"I was," Groucho assured me, "working up to that same question."

The young man took an uneasy step back from us. "I'll try to tell you all I know," he said in a very quiet voice. "But, you know, I won't tell anybody else. Not the police, I mean, or anybody like that."

Groucho nodded. "That's okay," he said. "With sufficient information, we can do what has to be done without involving you directly at all."

After a careful glance back at the closed door, Tristan inched closer to Groucho and addressed himself mainly to him. "I saw her body," he told him. "In the newspapers, you know, they said she'd killed herself by locking herself in the garage and leaving her car motor running." He shook his head slowly.

"You don't think that's what happened?"

The young man shook his head again. "I've been working here near two years," he went on, "and I've seen a lot of dead people. When you die from carbon monoxide poisoning, you know, your face turns really red." He paused, took a deep slow breath in and out. "Not her, not Miss McMorrow, no. You know, it's funny, but I saw her in a movie only a week or so ago. It was a cowboy picture and Tex Ritter was the—"

"What killed her, then?" asked Groucho.

Tristan glanced back at the door of the filing room once again. "She . . . damn," he said, wiping at his nose with his knuckles. "It's really hard to talk about it, Mr. Marx. I'm not supposed to go around the bodies, but a lot of times I do. I get scared working here alone at night, you know, and I'd quit if I didn't need the money so bad."

Groucho put his hand on his arm. "Take it easy, relax," he urged. "You think she was murdered? Is that it?"

He nodded, swallowing hard. "Her head was . . ." He touched his fingertips to his right temple. The whole hand was shaking. "All along the right side . . . it was, you know . . . it was smashed in and you could see—ow!"

Groucho had tightened his grip on the arm. "Sorry." He let go, muttering, "Bastards, the bastards."

"They must have hit her in the face, too, quite a lot," Tristan went on, voice husky and dim. "There were bruises on her face . . . here along the left cheek and down the right side. And, Jesus, I think they burned her, too. You know, with a cigarette or something . . . because all down the left arm there were these raw . . . Sorry, sorry." His head went forward and he start to cry softly. "Sorry, you know, I don't know why I'm crying."

"All right, okay," Groucho told him, his voice husky now, too. "You don't have to describe any more, Tristan."

The young man gave a grateful sigh and took a wrinkled white handkerchief out of his pocket. "All of that, you know, really upset me," he said. "It isn't right to pretend she killed herself, when I know damn well she didn't. But . . . you know, I can't do anything or I'll lose this job."

"You told us," said Groucho. "That's sufficient."

"Any idea," I asked the janitor, "who ordered Whitman to fake the death certificate?"

He wiped at his eyes, then blew his nose. "No, sir, I'm not sure," he answered. "Sergeant Branner, from the Bayside Police, was hanging around here a lot, but I'm not sure if he's the one or not."

Groucho nodded toward me. "Let's take our leave. I feel the need of fresh air."

"Yeah," I agreed. "Thanks, Tristan."

"You think maybe you can get them punished for what they did to her?"

"We can," said Groucho. "No maybe involved." He reached out and shook hands with the young man.

I shook hands next, telling him, "Don't show that autograph to anybody, okay?"

"Hell, I live by myself and I don't have a steady girl just now," he said. "You can bet I'm not going to show it to Mr. Whitman."

When we were outside in the chill night fog, Groucho took a fresh cigar out of his pocket, unwrapped it and then threw it violently away from him. "I always knew Hollywood was a lousy place," he said quietly. "But not this lousy."

Thirteen

The phone on the bedside table was ringing.

I sat up, nearly awake, and grabbed the receiver. "Hello?" I said in a somewhat blurred voice.

After what might be called a pregnant silence, a gruff male voice asked, "Who the hell are you?"

After yawning, I answered, "I might ask you the same question. You intrude on my sleep, then ask me a—"

"Honestly, Frank." Jane's bare arm reached over from the other side of the bed and, fairly gently, took the phone away from me. "Yes?"

I leaned against the backboard, remembering finally that I hadn't spent the night in my own bed. "Sorry," I said. "I only now realized that I—"

"Hush," she advised, making a shut-up gesture with her free hand.

Jane was wearing a simple sort of white sleeveless nightgown and no makeup and she looked great.

". . . a friend of mine who dropped over for breakfast, Rod," she was saying into the phone. "It's not the crack of dawn. It's nearly nine A.M. and . . . what? Well, the point is I can have anybody over to breakfast I damn well please."

"Is that Tommerlin?" I asked her, reaching for the phone. "Is he annoying you?"

"Everybody is annoying me at the moment. Shoo. Sit there with your hands folded and your yap buttoned tight," she said. "No, not you, Rod."

"Is he browbeating you?" I asked her.

Narrowing one eye and slapping her hand over the mouth-piece, Jane suggested, "Why don't you, please, take a vow of silence. This is strictly a *business* call."

I gave an exaggerated shrug, folded my arms and attempted to assume a dignified position. That is not especially easy to bring off when you've been sleeping in your underwear.

"I'm sorry to hear that, Rod," Jane said into the phone. "Of course, I'm sincere in my sympathy. Look, simply because a dear friend drops in for breakfast, that doesn't . . . Well, 'dear' means exactly that. No, he's not laughing at your misfortune. He's sitting here like a lump on a log, looking soulful. What? Well, in a chair. No, we're both sorry you have a bad chest cold, Rod."

Very quietly, I untangled myself from the blanket and the patchwork quilt.

". . . put about a teaspoon of eucalyptus oil in a pan of boil-ing water and inhale the fumes. No, it isn't a joke. My grand-mother used to do that whenever we had colds when I was a kid and it works wonders. Clears the lungs right up and . . . Huh? Well, she happens to be dead, but she lived to be eighty and she never in all her life sounded as clogged up as you do right now."

Free of the bed, I hurried over to the chair where I'd neatly left my clothes last night. Gathering them up in a quick bundle, I made my way out of the bedroom and into the breakfast nook.

". . . that's very thoughtful of you, Rod. Sure, I can finish the rest of the *Hillbilly Willie* promo stuff at my little studio here and bring it all over there tomorrow. What? Or, sure, the day after if you're not better by tomorrow. But, really, if you try that eucalyptus, you'll . . ."

I dressed swiftly in the narrow breakfast nook, with the venetian blind letting in a striped view of a stretch of morning beach and bright Pacific.

One of my argyle socks had disappeared overnight. Rather than intrude back into Jane's bedroom, I slipped my loafer on over my bare left foot.

There were two framed watercolors on the wall to my left. Very strong work, grim scenes of downtown Los Angeles at night. I leaned closer and, as I'd suspected, the signature was *Jane Danner.*

"I'm looking for a patron of the arts," she said behind me, "if you're interested."

"This one of Pershing Square is terrific."

"You sure you don't mean colossal."

I turned, grinning at her. "I never use Hollywood hyperbole to describe the work of those I am infatuated with at the moment," I assured her.

"Really it's just watered-down Reginald Marsh," Jane said, shrugging one shoulder.

"No, it's not."

"Well, thanks."

"No, it's more watered-down Edward Hopper. What did Rod Tommerlin want?"

"He's got, as you may've gathered while eavesdropping, a bad chest cold." She came into the breakfast nook and raised the venetian blind. "How come you aren't wearing socks?"

"I have one on."

"So you do. Would you like to do something wholesome today? Like a picnic or a drive up to Santa Barbara or a tour of the Missions?" she asked. "Rod says I ought to stay away from him today."

"Sure, fine," I said. "But I'd better check with my answering service first."

"You can use the phone in the living room while I get dressed."

There were three more watercolors in the small bright living room, all of them showing downtown L.A. at night.

I sat on the sofa and dialed my answering service. "This is Frank Denby."

"It's very exciting," said a slightly nasal voice. "I know I'm supposed to act blasé, because in this particular line of work we're liable to talk to dozens of celebrities and movie stars in any given day and it won't do to sound like some gushy tourist. But I've been a fan of his since I was this high and my folks took me to see him and his brothers on Broadway in *Animal Crackers* way back in—"

"Did Groucho Marx call me, Rita?"

"This isn't Rita, although you're not the first one today who's made that mistake. I'm Irene and I only started working here yesterday," she explained. "Yes, Mr. Marx phoned you at eight-fourteen A.M."

"Any message?"

"Here's exactly what he told me: Those halfwits from the ad agency want to see you two early this afternoon and to give him a ring as soon as you can."

"Any other messages?"

She hesitated a few seconds before saying, "Well, a Mr. Anderson phoned you at six twenty-two A.M."

I didn't recognize the name. "What'd he want?"

"I know I'm not supposed to get emotionally involved with our clients, nor am I to pass judgments," she said apologetically. "But I got to tell you, Mr. Denby, he sounded kind of spooky."

"Spooky?"

"Very cold and distant and . . . nasty," she answered. "I guess he works for a travel agency, but he sure doesn't have much of a telephone personality."

"What exactly did this guy say, Irene?"

"That he was Mr. Anderson and he wanted to suggest that you ought to take a trip out of town right away. For your health's sake, he said."

"I see, yeah. Is that about it for messages?"

"That's the lot, sorry. I know you were probably hoping that a zillion people phoned offering you jobs, but—"

"I've got all the jobs I can handle, thanks." After returning the receiver to its cradle, I leaned back and scanned the peach-colored stucco ceiling.

"We're not going to be able to spend the day together, are we?"

"Afraid not."

Jane was standing in the doorway, looking very pretty in tan slacks and a green pullover. "But that's not why you're looking that way. What's wrong, Frank?"

"Nothing serious. Just one of those annoying death threats."

She came hurrying over and sat beside me. "Damn it, you've got to stop playing detective. You and Groucho both," she told me, taking hold of my hand.

"I don't think we can stop, Jane," I said. "We have to keep going now just to find out who in the hell is trying to do us harm."

"That's a dumb attitude," she commented. "And I really hate to believe I'm falling for a man who's dumb."

I reached again for the phone. "I'd better phone Groucho."

"Tell him he's dumb, too."

I promised I would.

Fourteen

When the handsome blond man in the crimson jacket and gold trousers walked up and sneered at my Plymouth coupe, I realized that the afternoon was going to be even worse than I'd anticipated.

I could hear the babble of many voices and music, too. A group that was trying very hard to sound like Benny Goodman's quartet was playing "Avalon." Or maybe it actually was Goodman. Warren Stander, vice president for programming at NBN, could certainly afford the real one.

Groucho had informed me, when I'd phoned him from Jane's, that we'd been summoned to Stander's new mansion in Bel Air for a reading of the latest draft of the *Groucho Marx, Master Detective* script. It seemed that Junior Orem, our sponsor, had just arrived in Southern California and was eager to have the script read to him. If it wasn't too much trouble, it would be nice if Groucho and I would drop by Stander's place at around one P.M. and run through the thing for him. Nothing formal, you understand, no real actors except for Groucho.

I could do the rest of the parts. Just Stander and Orem and Jape Griffin, the account executive, and a few other toadies and hangers-on were going to sit in on the reading.

"This whole thing is giving me a severe pain in the fanny," Groucho had confided that morning. "But, foolish little thing that I am, I seem to have developed this morbid fascination with money. My ne'er-do-well brother Chico is always borrowing it to pay off a pack of gamblers, my wife requires heaps of it—and, hell, I can use the stuff myself, if you must know. I appreciate the fact that you're reluctant to tear yourself away from Mistress Danner, especially in light of the lewd things you probably did to her all through the night and if you didn't do lewd things you ought to have your head examined, which our organization will be more than glad to do for you if you will simply wrap the head in sturdy brown paper, tie it with sturdy brown twine and ship it to our Pasadena office. Mark it all over *Musk Melons! Fragile!* And then, in red crayon scrawl *S.W.A.K.* That means Sealed With A Kiss and will prompt Mr. Mulrooney in shipping to get off his . . . Where was I?"

"About six miles out of Altoona, the last time we got a report from the weather bureau."

"Oh, it all comes back to me now," said Groucho. "Meet me at Warren Stander's new eyesore in Bel Air at about one-ish. We'll whiz through the script, take a bow, pass the hat and get the hell out of there. Unpleasant, to be sure, but one of the things that must be done. We'll get back to the case later on today."

"Speaking of that, I—"

"I must be going," he'd said and hung up.

At a few minutes shy of one that afternoon the big blond parking attendant was urging me out of my car. "I'll park this behind some shrubbery so no one will see it, sir," he said, taking my place at the wheel. "Save us both a lot of embarrassment."

From the sound of it, the group that had gathered to hear the script read had grown substantially. Giving a resigned sigh, I watched my car go rattling off down the white curving drive and disappear. Then I climbed up a twisting marble staircase, through a density of tropical plants and trees and along a broad path that skirted Stander's vaguely Moorish mansion.

It *was* Benny Goodman, as well as Teddy Wilson, Gene Krupa and Lionel Hampton. They were playing on a bandstand that had been set up on the wide expanse of extremely green lawn that went stretching away from the far side of the Olympic-size swimming pool.

There were at least two hundred people back there, wandering the grounds, using the pool and patronizing the bar that had been set up in an ornate gazebo just to the left of the music.

I noticed Jack Benny having a very serious conversation with Edgar Bergen. Joan Blondell was hugging somebody I think was a stuntman over at Warner's. Cesar Romero was apparently demonstrating how to do a handstand for a circle of women that included Carole Lombard, Pauline Moore, Hedda Hopper and Patsy Kelly. Mickey Rooney, wearing a pair of somewhat droopy swim trunks, was climbing up on the bandstand and looked to be trying to persuade Krupa to let him sit in on the drums.

Chester Morris, wearing a very handsome double-breasted

pin-stripe suit, came up and shook my hand. "Good luck on the new show, kid," he said.

"You're looking very dapper."

"It's in my contract."

"Seen Groucho?"

"Down by the gazebo a minute ago."

We shook hands again and I headed for the outdoor bar. There were no fewer than three red-coated bartenders up there mixing drinks for a crowd of about forty people. Groucho, however, was at the foot of the stairs leading up to the bar, a large yellow daisy tucked behind his left ear.

A handsome middle-aged woman in a flowered tea dress and picture hat was on the first step, smiling down at him.

I hurried down there. "Hello, Miss Dumont," I said to the actress. "Groucho, I thought you told me we were going to do this for maybe a dozen people."

"The situation got somewhat out of hand."

"I can read that stuff in a meeting room with a bunch of executives maybe," I told him. "But not in front of a show business crowd. I'm not an actor or—"

"You could be," he told me, placing both hands over his heart, "the noblest actor of your generation, sonny boy, if only you'd pay more attention to your elocution lessons. Or even your electrocution lessons for that matter." He sighed deeply, batting his eyelashes. "Why I was chatting, tête-à-tête to be sure, with De Mille only the other day about you. That's Abe De Mille who runs a kosher delicatessen on Spring Street. 'Gummo,' he said, mistaking me for one of my less toothsome brothers, 'that Denby lad has the makings of a great thespian if only he'd pay more attention to his elocution.' I avoided the obvious plays on words connected with the word thespian and he continued his discourse. 'Gumbo,' he said, this time mistaking me for a bowl of soup, 'you ought to get that lad to read from a radio script up on a platform in front of a horde of drunken, oversexed cinemactors.' With which sentiment I heartily concur. I concluded our inspiring conversation by advising him that he'd never prosper so long as he tries to operate a delicatessen in the heart of Chinatown."

Margaret Dumont gave me a sympathetic look. "Nothing can be done about him," she said quietly.

Nodding, I asked him, "When are we supposed to stage this fiasco?"

"As soon as Junior Orem arrives."

"He's not here yet?"

"I believe he went out for a cup of coffee and is expected back shortly."

"If Miss Dumont will excuse you, I want to talk to you in private, Groucho."

She made a dismissive gesture. "You're more than welcome to him."

I started moving away from the gazebo and Groucho followed. "What's bothering you, Rollo? You appear to . . . Ah, good afternoon, Myrna. Good afternoon, Eleanor. Good afternoon, Joan."

Myrna Loy, Eleanor Powell and Joan Crawford, each clad in a bright tea dress, came walking by arm in arm.

Loy smiled at him. Powell smiled, too. But from Crawford there was only a fleeting and disdainful glance.

Groucho pursed his lips. "Joan has never fully recuperated from that incident in the phone booth," he remarked with a sad shake of his head. "There's a mammoth greenhouse down behind that stand of pine trees yonder. Is this about Peg?"

"About her and about me," I said.

"We'll have oodles of privacy there," he assured me. "Not to mention hay fever."

Fifteen

But that means we're making progress," insisted Groucho as we strolled along a lane between rows of potted flowers. "These scoundrels wouldn't be harassing you if we weren't getting closer to nabbing them."

"Harassing is maybe too mild a term to use in describing death threats," I mentioned.

He slowed, glancing up at the curved, glass-paneled ceiling far above us. "This is getting risky," he conceded. "In fact, if you want to quit the team, why, I'll carry on alone and you—"

"I didn't say a damn thing about quitting," I told him. "But I have to admit that message from Mr. Anderson unsettled me."

"Be interesting to find out who Anderson really is."

We passed into the second section of the large greenhouse. They grew tropical plants in there, as well as potted palm trees and, all along one wall, a large thick stand of high green bamboo.

"This smells like a Tarzan set," observed Groucho. "Except there's no monkey crap underfoot. Did you know that schmuck chimpanzee used to bite Maureen O'Sullivan when she was playing the apeman's mate in those things?"

"I also heard you were waiting in line right behind the chimp."

Groucho's eyebrows rose and he assumed an innocent expression. "You should know better than to believe what you read in the gossip columns, Rollo," he said. "Surely you don't think I'd so much as flirt with a married woman?"

"Um," I replied. "We'd better get together after my public humiliation and work out what we're going to do next on this case."

"Precisely what I was about to suggest," he said. "I probably should be the one to call on that swish decorator, LaSalle. I can pretend I want my billiard room refurbished."

"Yeah, I don't think he'd be interested in working on my place."

"Not unless he does fumigating on the side, no," Groucho remarked. "It's my hunch that LaSalle was just fronting for somebody else when he sprang for the cremation." His slouch increased and his pace slowed. "Do you think it's possible Peg was blackmailing someone?"

I said, "Yes."

"If she had some incriminating stuff hidden someplace," Groucho suggested, "then that would explain . . . explain why she was tortured before she died. To make her tell them where."

"We're already pretty sure they were looking for something like letters or photos."

Halting on the graveled hothouse path, Groucho absently tugged out a new cigar. "Did they ransack her cottage before or after they killed her?"

I thought about it. "Probably before."

"That's what I've been thinking," he said. "They search the house, looking for something. But they don't find it, so they . . . they try to make her tell them where it's hidden."

I said, "Of course, there is the possibility that she refused to tell and *then* they tore the place apart looking."

"No, my theory is that they didn't intend to kill her as soon as they did," Groucho said. "Somebody hit her too hard and . . ." He looked down, sighed. "Jesus, Frank, listen to me. I'm starting to sound so damned matter-of-fact about her death, chatting about it like some stooge in a Charlie Chan movie."

"If we're going to find out who killed Peg," I reminded him, "then you can't afford to get sentimental about her. Not this far along, Groucho."

He nodded and started walking again. After nearly a minute, he said, "Seems to me there's a strong possibility that they never did find what they were looking for. That would explain their taking potshots at us and threatening you. They don't have it and they're afraid we'll find it."

"We'd be a hell of a lot further along if we knew what *it* actually is."

"My vote goes for photographs, considering that her cameras and all her photo albums are missing."

"Yeah, incriminating photos is a good bet," I acknowledged. "But it still could be something else. Or a combination of pictures and something else besides."

Groucho suddenly stopped in his tracks, putting out his arm to block my progress. "Over in that bamboo yonder," he said softly. "I'm damned sure somebody's lurking in—"

A pistol was fired then. Twice.

Glass shattered, somebody groaned.

The high bamboo rattled and swayed. There was a lot of thrashing and crashing.

A wide dark man in a gray suit came staggering out of the bamboo, a .45 automatic dangling in his right hand.

"Dirty son . . ." He was muttering, blood starting to spurt out with his words. "Dirty son of a . . ."

He dropped to his knees on the gravel of the pathway.

He finally got the whole phrase out. "Dirty son of a bitch."

After that he let go of the gun, toppled forward on his face and died.

Groucho stood up and away from the body.

Five or six minutes had passed since the two slugs went into the man's back and killed him. Apparently the noise of the party a few acres uphill from the greenhouse had drowned out the sound of the shots and of the glass panels shattering. At least, nobody had come down here.

"Not a speck of identification." Groucho took out his pocket handkerchief and wiped at his hands. "Now I move we flee the scene of the crime."

"And just leave him here?"

"You'd perhaps prefer to stick around, give this lout a state funeral and afterwards a twenty-one-gun salute?"

I answered, "Nope, there's no use in our getting mixed up with the police just yet."

"I'm content to let someone else find him, the later the better." He turned on his heel and headed back the way we'd come.

I caught up with him. "Still, it seems sort of callous to me."

"He was almost certainly the latest in what I hope won't be a long line of goons sent to use us for target practice, my boy." Groucho increased his pace. "Let me further point out, Rollo, that whoever shot him up may well still be in the vicinity. Yet another perfectly good reason to hotfoot it elsewhere."

"It occurs to me that whoever shot this guy may have been doing it to keep him from shooting us."

"A gun-toting guardian angel, huh?"

"Somebody looking after us, yeah."

He hesitated at the exit and then pushed the door slowly open. "There's a decided lack of privacy in a greenhouse. Have you noticed that?" he remarked. "Also, if I lived in one I don't think I'd do much in the way of throwing stones."

I followed him out into the bright afternoon, glancing carefully around us. There was no sign of anyone. From up near the mansion drifted the sound of Goodman's group playing "Sweet Georgia Brown."

"Could that dead chap have been Anderson?" asked Groucho as we started up toward the noise of the party.

"Might've been."

"Hell, he might've been Judge Crater." Groucho scowled. "Little too young to be the Lindbergh baby, but you never can tell."

"Okay, let's assume, whoever he was, that he was tailing us," I said. "He may've had orders to shoot us or simply to scare us or—"

"He succeeded in that. I've been scared for . . . oh, a good fifteen minutes now."

"What we have to figure out is who he was working for."

"Obviously the bunch who killed Peg."

"Then who killed *him?*"

"One might also ask, especially if one wanted to drive one's self stark raving bonkers, why there seem to be two different groups of thugs, at least, involved in this mess."

I said, "Of course, there's always the possibility that this has nothing whatsoever to do with us or with Peg."

"Oh, so?"

"I mean, maybe this guy ran into one of his creditors at the party. Or he was fooling around with somebody's wife and the irate husband caught up with him in the hothouse."

"They don't shoot adulterers in this town. If they did, I'd have more holes in me than a swiss cheese by now."

"The trouble is we don't know enough about the damned gunman to even—"

"So there you jerks are." Jape Griffin, the account exec on Orem Bros. Coffee, was trotting down toward us.

Drawing himself up to his full height, Groucho pointed an admonishing finger at him. "I resent deeply, sir, the term jerks," he said. "That is, I resent your using it in the plural. My associate, as I've long suspected, may well be a jerk. I, however, am known in academic circles—and I've been going around in academic circles so long that I'm getting terribly dizzy—I, have a care, am known far and wide—or is it wide and far? Be that as it may, all is forgiven and the curfew shall not ring tonight. But keep next Tuesday open."

"I hope to god you're going to be funnier than that when you read the goddamn script to this bunch," said Jape forlornly. "Speaking of which, you were due to start ten minutes ago. Where the hell were you?"

Groucho unwrapped a new cigar. "It was such an absolutely gorgeous day, Jape, that we couldn't keep from gamboling on the sward," he said. "We were also contemplating trying a little Morris dancing, but Morris's tootsies are bothering him something awful. Now if you're completely through babbling, lead us, if you will, to the scene of our upcoming triumph."

After making an exasperated noise, the big account man said, "Come on, gentlemen."

"Watch who you're calling a gentleman." Groucho lit his cigar.

As I should have anticipated, the reading of my script was a definite hit. That was due in large part to Groucho. I'd never seen him work with an audience before and I hadn't realized how that buoyed him up. It even, somehow, seemed to improve the material.

About a hundred or more of Warren Stander's guests were crowded into the beam-ceilinged music room to hear us run through the half-hour radio play. Junior Orem, a lank, leathery man, shared a loveseat with Jape Griffin up near our improvised stage.

Before we ever got around to the actual script, though, Groucho did some performing on his own. It turned out he'd brought along his guitar, something I wasn't even aware of until he hopped up on the small rectangular stage clutching it. He opened with a medley of songs from the Marx Brothers movies, including "Ev'ry One Says 'I Love You' " from *Horse Feathers* and "The Monkey Doodle-Doo" from *The Cocoanuts.* For an encore he led everybody in a rendition of the Captain Spalding song from *Animal Crackers.* When I noticed Junior Orem clapping his hands and laughing during that one, I experienced something approaching optimism.

Groucho's second medley consisted of Gilbert and Sullivan material, mostly from his favorite, *The Mikado.*

By the time I joined him to deliver the script, that audience of movie people and businessmen was gratifyingly receptive. Groucho had persuaded Margaret Dumont to read the part of the rich client, Mrs. Uppercase, and she did a perfect job. For good measure, Carole Lombard, admittedly a shade tipsy by that time, played our femme fatale. Mickey Rooney insisted on being the detective agency office boy and we allowed him to do that, but only after he agreed not to borrow Krupa's drums and add a drum solo to the reading. I took the five other speaking parts and provided the simpler sound effects. I sounded pretty good at everything except the Swedish maid.

Chester Morris shook my hand again as I was leaving the music room. "Not bad for an amateur, kid," he said. "But I'd stick to the writing. That you do pretty good."

I departed and retrieved my car from its hiding place amid

the shrubbery on a little side lane. I climbed in and headed home for Bayside. I was going to have an early dinner with Jane, then meet Groucho at his place in Beverly Hills.

Little did I know what was actually going to befall me.

Sixteen

Groucho, he later told me, had lingered at the mansion after our performance and dusk was spreading through the Rodeo Drive area of Beverly Hills when he parked his car on a narrow side street. Since the oncoming evening was warm, he left his houndstooth sport coat draped on the passenger seat and went forth in his short-sleeved shirt, which was just about the color of lemon sherbet.

Several of the shops along the Drive were still open and their lights were coming on, with early diners already drifting into the latest fashionable little restaurants. At the corner a large gray-haired woman noticed Groucho, did a gratified take and commenced producing the familiar sounds of recognition.

"Mr. Marx," she said, approaching him while he waited for the light to change. "I simply adore you."

After glancing furtively around, Groucho hunched slightly and said, "Eunice, what did I tell you about following me around like this and declaring your mad passion for me?"

She blinked, puzzled. "Oh, I don't happen to be this Eunice," she assured him. "I'm Rena Valerio from Woodland Hills, in town for a shopping—"

"Eunice, the good lord knows I've struggled mightily to fight this burning desire I have for you," he continued. "But seeing you like this again . . . And, by the by, what happened to your vow to renounce the sins of the flesh and enter a convent? Well, I suppose with that much flesh, it proved to be too much of a chore." He chuckled, slipping an arm around her ample waist. "I take it Dr. Kammerman knows you're loose? Well, no matter, let's make the most of—"

"Please, Mr. Marx." She struggled to get free. "You, really now, have me mixed up with someone else."

"I've got *you* mixed up? How do you think *I* must feel, Eunice? Knowing that you're dying of euphonic plague, knowing as well that I probably caught it from you and have only months to—"

"Nice meeting you, Mr. Marx." She pulled free of him to go hurrying away into the gathering twilight. "I do like you in the movies, though."

Groucho fetched out a cigar and crossed the street against the signal.

The lights were on in the interior decorating establishment. In the narrow display window sat the skeleton of a single unupholstered armchair. There was a partially unfurled bolt of crimson silk leaning against the chair and five paper roses were scattered around its raw wood legs. Inscribed low on the glass door in very small gilded italics was the name *Justin LaSalle.*

Groucho entered the stark reception room. It contained a

small potted palm in an ebony pot, a white desk and chair and a very blond receptionist in a starkly simple black frock.

"Yes?" she inquired, looking briefly up from the thick, slick architectural magazine she was leafing through.

"I want to see LaSalle," he informed her.

"That's highly unlikely," she said, returning her attention to the magazine.

"Oh, so?" Crossing the black and white floor, Groucho perched on the edge of her desk. "I'm especially eager to do business with him."

"You and half the other misguided dimwits in this town."

"Suppose you tell him I'm here?" he suggested. "You probably don't recognize me without my makeup, but I'm Lionel Barrymore and I'd like to have LaSalle redecorate my sister Ethel and—"

"You're, in point of fact, Groucho Marx, which is bad enough." She grimaced at him. *"John* Barrymore was in here a few days back and he pinched my rear end, relieved himself in that pot yonder and then went to sleep on Mr. LaSalle's drawing table."

"Yes, Jack's an awful lot of fun, isn't he? Where's LaSalle?"

"Away," she said.

"Are you ordering me to go away or telling me that LaSalle is away?"

"He's in Florida."

"Whereabouts in Florida? As I recall they have several different towns down there."

"He didn't confide in me."

"How can I contact him?"

She shrugged. "Beats me."

"Okay, when is he due back from Florida?"

"It's my impression that Mr. LaSalle will be out of town for quite some time."

"Left in a hurry, did he?"

Nodding, she once again turned to the open magazine.

Groucho leaned closer. "Perhaps, then, you can help me," he suggested.

"Not much of a chance of that."

"Give it a try. After all, the bridge is out and we're likely to be stranded here until the next thaw," he said. "Answering some questions will help pass the time away."

She said nothing.

"I was," continued Groucho, "a friend of Peg McMorrow's. What I'd like to—"

"You don't want to ask questions about that McMorrow girl." She shut the magazine and stood up.

"I'm curious as to why LaSalle paid to have her cremated. Were they friends or did someone else ask—"

"The reason Mr. LaSalle is out of town, if you want my opinion, is because of this McMorrow business."

"I agree. If you could provide some details or tell me why you suspect—"

"We're closing for the day." She picked up a small black purse from the side of the white desk.

"Did someone send LaSalle down there—or did he decide to skip town?"

"That's all I can tell you," she said. "You wouldn't want me to start screaming and then tell whoever comes running that you made an obscene proposal to me, would you?"

"I'd probably have to work long and hard to come up with

a proposal that *you'd* find obscene, my child," he said, then shrugged. "But we may as well avoid a scene. Good evening." He tipped an imaginary hat and went strolling out into the dusk.

Groucho was still a half block from his car when a man who could probably have gotten work doubling for Clark Gable came up beside him.

"Mr. Marx," he said quietly.

"Okay, where's your autograph book?"

"Probably in the attic in my grandmother's farmhouse up in Fresno." He jabbed a gun into Groucho's right side. "Walk right on by your car and climb into that gray Cadillac at the corner."

"If it's all the same with you, I'd just as soon start running as fast as my little legs can carry me," countered Groucho. "I suddenly remembered that my doctor advised me to get plenty of sleep, fresh air and exercise. So, if you don't mind, I'll—"

"Beverly Hills is a fairly conservative place, Mr. Marx." The pressure from the barrel of the gun increased. "They get very angry and upset every time I shoot down somebody on their streets. But if you don't get your ass in that Cadillac right now, I'm going to have to—"

"I'll get in your car," said Groucho obligingly. "I can run twice as far tomorrow."

Seventeen

There was a chill wind blowing in off the night Pacific. Standing on the private wharf, Groucho shivered and said, "I wish you lads had allowed me to gather my jacket."

"Here." The large thickset man standing close on his left shrugged out of his camel hair overcoat. "Put this goddamn thing on and quit bellyaching."

"Oh, that's all right. It'd be easier if you just run me back to Beverly Hills to—"

"Put it on."

Groucho got into the coat, which came down over his ankles. "Harpo would have fun filling this with silverware, but for myself—"

"You can climb into the launch now," instructed the one who resembled Gable.

"You know, fellows, my horoscope just this morning warned against a sea voyage of any sort," Groucho told them, not budging. "So if it's all the same with you, I'll sit this one—"

"Move it." The one who'd loaned him his overcoat gave

Groucho a helpful flat-handed shove in the back to propel him on his way.

Stumbling ahead, Groucho stepped down into the motor launch that was moored below.

Out across the dark ocean the lights of the *Encantada* gambling ship sparkled, intensely yellow, in the clear, crisp night. At the next wharf over, several water taxis were bobbing in the dark water. It was too early yet for any of the ship's customers to be heading out for an evening of roulette, faro and craps.

The two heavies bookended Groucho on the passenger seat. A silent Negro cast off and piloted the launch away from the Santa Monica wharf. It inscribed a foamy half arc on the night water and then headed toward the lights of the ship.

The trip out to the *Encantada* took nearly a half hour. When they arrived alongside the huge ship, the thickset man went up the dangling gangway first. Then Groucho climbed it, followed by the roadshow Gable.

On the deck, just inside the rail, a fat man in an oil-stained sweatshirt reached for Groucho. "Got to frisk you, sweetheart," he explained.

"He's clean," said the thickset man.

"C'mon, Maury, it's my ass if I don't pat everybody down." He made a chesty chuckling noise while he ran his big hands over Groucho.

"You can guess my weight if you'd like," Groucho invited.

The fat man asked, "What is this guy—a comedian?"

"He sure thinks so." Maury held out his left hand as soon as the fat man finished his work. "The coat."

Slipping free of it, Groucho handed it over. "Have it short-ened some and it could use—maybe, mind you—a little less padding in the shoulders. If you had the same thing in a flow-ered print, why I'd—"

"Go along to your right now," the other gunman told him.

As Groucho made his way along the deck, a metal door swung open and blocked his path.

"In there."

Groucho went in.

I awakened in darkness, a thick surrounding darkness that smelled thickly of oil, salt water and sea food that was long past its prime.

The back of my head, from about the top of my skull to the low point of my neck, hurt and throbbed. The gentle rocking I now became aware of didn't help much. I felt extremely un-settled inside, experiencing something that reminded me of a bad blend of a hangover and a bout of influenza.

"Jesus," I remarked and noticed that my voice was a dry croak.

A door opened with a metallic creak and showed a rectan-gle of night and a lean man wearing a peacoat and a knit cap. "Time to rise and shine, mate," he suggested in an uncon-vincing British accent.

He crossed into the cabin and flicked on the overhead lights. I had the brief and painful impression that someone was trying to force both my eyeballs back into my skull.

"Up and at 'em, sonny boy." The sailor came over to the bunk I was sprawled on, took hold of my nearest elbow and tugged me up into a sitting position. "Quite a goose egg you've collected on your sconce, mate."

"Didn't you used to play bit parts over at Mascot?"

"Matter of fact, I did."

"I thought I recognized that imitation limey accent of yours." I sat there for a moment, legs hanging down and both hands gripping the edge of the metal bed frame.

"This job pays much better, if you want the truth."

"I figured as much, having seen you try to act," I said, my voice getting some of its old qualities back. "Where am I supposed to be going?"

"Somebody wants to see you chop chop."

I took a couple of deep breaths in through my open mouth. "How far out at sea are we?"

"Just far enough to gamble legally, mate."

"So this is the *Encantada?*"

"That she is."

After another breath, I stood up. My left leg gave out entirely and I started to fall.

The sailor caught my arm and kept me from dropping to the cabin floor. "Getting sapped'll do this to you sometimes," he told me. "You'll be shipshape again soon enough, never fear."

"Actually, I'm not all that sure I want to be shipshape."

He guided me toward the open doorway. "Well, let's get underway," he said. "Can't keep 'em waiting, can we?"

Eighteen

Vince Salermo was a small, compact man, not more than five foot four. He was deeply tanned, nearly bald and in his early fifties. His double-breasted suit was a midnight black. Salermo's office aboard the *Encantada* was large and without a desk.

The gambler, smiling, sat in a leather armchair at the left of the room. A lean blond man, considerably younger than Salermo, leaned against the wall near a porthole. A third man, large and wide, stood just to the rear of the leather chair with both hands in his trouser pockets.

Groucho, in his shirt sleeves, was sitting in a folding metal chair facing Salermo. When I was shoved into the office, he stood up and scrutinized me. "Are you that strange green shade because you're seasick?" he asked me.

"I think it's mostly from being bopped on the head with a blackjack."

Turning toward the gangster, Groucho said, "I've been behaving in my usual amiable fashion thus far, Salermo. And you've been telling me this is just supposed to be a friendly get-together."

"It is, Groucho. Relax." He spread his small hands wide, smiling more broadly.

"It's bad enough you kidnapped me," continued Groucho, angry. "But you also kidnap my friend and associate here—and then rough him up."

"Please, Groucho," said Salermo. "I've been trying to explain that you and Denby weren't supposed to be harmed. I told my people simply to invite you over for a friendly chat."

Ignoring him, Groucho came over to where I was standing. "Are you okay?"

"More or less," I answered, feeling gingerly at the bump on my head. "Two of them were waiting for me when I got home from Bel Air. When I refused to go anyplace with them, the larger one bopped me with—"

"You came near to busting Eddie's nose when you swung on him," Salermo said, still smiling, though not as broadly. "I'm not saying, Groucho, that Eddie didn't exceed his authority in the matter. But surely you can see how he got temporarily angry and lost control of—"

"What I see is that you fellows could end up in Alcatraz for kidnapping."

Salermo glanced over at the younger man. "Did you hear that, Bud?" They both laughed. "You'll never prove anything like that," he said. "Not in California."

"They all think Mr. Salermo is a saint hereabouts," Bud added.

Groucho gave an annoyed sigh and nodded at the chair. "Sit down, Frank."

"Thanks." It was the only chair in the room besides Salermo's, so I dropped into it.

Groucho turned to the gangster. "Okay, this wasn't a kidnapping, you didn't slug my friend," he began. "Suppose you tell us now why the hell we're here."

"That's exactly what I've been trying to do, Groucho," Salermo said. "It recently came to my attention that you were interested in the same unfortunate young lady that we are."

"Peg McMorrow," I said quietly.

Groucho took a step in the gangster's direction. "What did you have to do with her death, Salermo?"

Salermo held up his left hand and made a stop-right-there gesture. "Hey, you're missing the point," he said. "From what I've been hearing, Groucho, you don't believe the girl committed suicide."

"I don't, no."

"We don't think so either," continued the gambler. "Who do you think killed Peggy and passed it off as a suicide?"

"We haven't gotten that far yet," Groucho answered. "But you're supposed to have a fairly cordial relationship with the law. They know a hell of a lot more about Peg McMorrow's death than we do at the moment, Salermo. Why not ask them to show you what—"

"I'm working on that angle, too," said Salermo. "Trouble is, Groucho, the cops in Bayside aren't as cordially disposed toward me as the cops in some of the other towns around here. In fact, a few bastards on the Bayside force hate my guts."

"Sergeant Branner," Bud muttered, making a spitting noise.

I rubbed at the back of my head again and asked Salermo, "Why are you interested in Peg McMorrow at all?"

"I liked the kid, in a purely avuncular way," he replied.

"She came out here to the boat a few times with Shel Leverson, a business associate of mine."

"She was going with him," said Groucho.

"Not recently. They broke up a while back, but naturally Shel's concerned about what's happened."

"Why isn't he at our little powwow?"

"He wanted to be, Groucho, but he had to go down to Mexico yesterday on important business. Naturally I'll tell him whatever I find out."

"She was out here on the *Encantada* just a few nights ago," said Groucho.

Salermo shook his head. "No, that's not true, Groucho. Is it, Bud?"

"No, Peggy hasn't been around here for a hell of a long while."

Groucho's eyebrows rose and fell. "All right, Salermo, she wasn't here," he said. "Suppose you tell me your theories about what happened?"

"To put your mind at ease," he said, smiling, "I didn't invite you guys out here to sell you a line of crap, Groucho. What I mean is, we didn't kill her, nobody associated with me killed her. I really am interested in the truth here—I want to know who killed the kid."

"Rivals of yours maybe?"

"Possibly, but I doubt it."

"Who then?"

"We don't know yet," admitted Salermo. "Maybe some of her movie friends, maybe some bastard she gave the cold shoulder to. I want you to tell me what you've dug up so far."

Groucho moved nearer my chair and rested his right hand on the back of it. "We haven't come up with much of anything yet," he told the gangster. "And, I must tell you, Salermo, that being kidnapped by goons and taken on long ocean trips is simply going to interfere with any sort of investigating we are doing."

"It won't happen again." He stopped smiling, studying Groucho's face. "You really haven't found out much?"

"Little of value," Groucho said. He let go of the chair, took a few sliding steps to the right. "I hope you won't think me unreasonably curious, but have you had us followed in recent days?"

Salermo said, "I instructed a few of my associates to keep an eye on you."

"Did one of them telephone me," I asked, "and suggest I get out of town?"

The gambler shook his head. "Nobody was told to threaten either one of you," he assured us.

"And you didn't send a lad with a forty-five to take a few shots at us this afternoon?"

"You have my word."

"Then did the chap you had watching us happen to spot him?"

Salermo coughed into his fist. "You fellows are looking tired, Groucho," he said, nodding toward Bud. "See that they get run back to shore and taken home. And no rough stuff, understand?"

"Absolutely not," Bud said.

Salermo remained in his chair as Groucho helped me up. "We'll keep in touch, Groucho," he said, smiling. "And I hope there are no hard feelings. After all, we're on the same side in this."

"Why should we have hard feelings about being kidnapped and beaten?" asked Groucho, smiling a smile that was a parody of Salermo's.

Bud crossed over to open the door of the cabin. "C'mon," he said to us.

Salermo called, "By the way, what's the title of your next movie, Groucho?"

"20,000 Years in Sing Sing," answered Groucho and stepped out onto the deck.

Nineteen

I was in the bathroom, trying to get a view of the back of my head by using the mirror in the medicine cabinet door and one of Jane's hand mirrors.

"Hey, get in here quick," she called.

I spun, causing my head to suffer a zigzag burst of pain, and ran to the breakfast nook. "What's wrong?"

She pointed at the portable radio that was sitting atop the breakfast table.

Johnny Whistler was doing his regular Hollywood segment on the morning news hour. ". . . And now, as I promised before the commercial break, friends, a word about Groucho's upcoming venture upon the kilowatts. Broadcast execs, and those in the know in radioland, are predicting that *Groucho Marx, Master Detective,* is going to be one of the top new shows of the season," the gossip was saying in that piping voice of his. "A sneak reading of the script for a select audience of Tinseltown celebrities and radio moguls yesterday at a palatial Hollywood mansion, so my sources inform me, was a decided hit. So good luck to you, Groucho. You've always been my favorite Marx Brother . . . Over at Monarch Studios, so we hear . . ."

Jane reached out to turn off the radio, but I caught her hand. "I want to hear this."

". . . the often grumpy studio boss, Eli Kurtzman, is smiling from here to here. Reason why? Well, the sneak preview the other P.M. of the new Tom Kerry swashbuckler, *The Pirate Prince,* got a one hundred percent enthusiastic response from the audience. Looks like it'll be the biggest box office hit yet for the dashing Kerry . . . Speaking of the Marx clan, Harpo, the one who doesn't talk much, is giving a harp concert this Friday eve in the Hollywood Bowl and, so they tell me, it's sold out already . . . And here's a word of caution to George Raft. George, I'm one of your biggest supporters, but—"

I clicked off the radio. "Enough of that."

She went back to setting the table for breakfast. "Why the interest in old Kurtzman?"

"There's a possibility," I said as I headed for the small kitchen, "that Peg McMorrow was in the midst of making some sort of deal with Monarch when she was killed."

Jane caught up with me as I was reaching for the perking coffee pot. "Don't you pay a damn bit of attention to anything I say to you?" There was both annoyance and anger in her voice.

"Your every word is indelibly engraved on the tablet of my memory and—"

"And quit talking like Groucho."

"Groucho would never respond that mildly and gently to such violent nagging. Honestly, Jane, I don't see—"

"You come dragging over here last night, hours late as usual. You've got a fractured skull and all sorts of other—"

"Bump," I corrected, turning the gas down under the coffee. "All I got was a bad bump on the skull."

"Furthermore, you looked like you'd been swimming in a sewer, you'd been abducted by gangsters. But now you—"

"Possibly I exaggerated a little, to get your sympathy," I told her.

"What I told you last night, Frank, I still believe this morning," Jane said, unsmiling. "You absolutely have to drop this whole mess right now." She crossed to a cabinet and yanked out two coffee cups. "You've been shot at, beaten, kidnapped, threatened. That's plenty. Quit, please."

"I admit that some unsettling things have happened to me since I started working on this case," I conceded. "But I'm more than ever convinced that Peg McMorrow was murdered. I can't drop this now. I can't let Groucho down."

"Groucho's a millionaire, isn't he? Tell him to go hire a private detective to do his dirty work. Hell, he can probably afford to hire a whole detective agency. There's no reason he has to send a bumbling amateur out to risk—"

"Whoa now," I cut in. "I did get shot at and hit on the head, granted. But that sort of stuff happens to professional operatives, too. And for quite a long time, damn it, Jane, I was a pretty good reporter who wasn't afraid to—"

"You don't have to yell at me in my own house," she yelled. "I'm trying to keep you alive, you damn idiot."

"I think I'll go now."

"You haven't had breakfast."

"Even so."

"Well, at least stop long enough to put on your shoes."

I looked down at my bare feet. "Okay, and I might as well at least have a cup of coffee." I smiled tentatively at her.

She smiled back and then carried the two cups into the breakfast nook.

At about the same time that Jane was trying to persuade me not to get killed, Groucho was sitting in the den of his Beverly Hills home. As happened often, his family had scattered and, except for a couple of servants, he had the place pretty much to himself.

Using a legal tablet he'd bought two days ago in a dime store in Westwood Village and a fountain pen he'd borrowed from his attorney last autumn and never returned, Groucho was making notes on the Peg McMorrow case. "How much does Salermo know?" he was asking himself while doodling in the margin. "One of his thugs must've shot that goon who was going to pot us in the greenhouse. But who hired *him?* And here's another pertinent question—What's the capital of North Dakota?"

The telephone atop the desk rang.

Grabbing up the receiver, Groucho said, "Sixth Day Adventist Headquarters. Call us back in a couple of days, when we hope to have graduated to Seventh Day—"

"Is that you, Mr. Marx?" asked a young woman's voice.

"Sally?" He sat up straighter in his chair.

Sally St. Clair said, "You told me to telephone you if I thought of anything about Peg."

"That's right. Have you got something?"

"This isn't exactly something I thought of, but it could be important, Mr. Marx."

Nodding, he said, "Okay, tell me."

"Well, I don't know if you remember Hulda Bjornsen, but—"

"She used to be a maid at the Young Actresses' Club, didn't she? Peg and she were friends, as I recall."

"That's right," said Sally. "Hulda is still working there and she happened to come into Marcus's Department Store, to the section where I work, on her day off yesterday."

"Uh-huh?"

"Anyhow, Mr. Marx, we talked about poor Peg and Hulda told me she saw Peg just the other night. Peg telephoned her, after they hadn't seen each other for months and they got together for dinner."

"At the True Blue Cafeteria," supplied Groucho.

"Oh, then you already know about all this?"

"Nope, I only knew that Peg had eaten there. No details as to who or why."

"I really think you should talk to Hulda. I have a hunch Peg gave Hulda something to keep for her," said Sally. "You know, something important that she was concerned about. My feeling is that Peg made that dinner date with Hulda—and Hulda is somebody everybody trusts—just so she could give her something to look after for her."

"Did she actually tell you that?"

"No, not directly, Mr. Marx. But when I asked her if Peg had entrusted something to her, she got very flustered and then started talking about something else," answered Sally. "You really ought to look her up. She might confide in you."

"Is she working at the place today?"

"As far as I know."

"I'll drop around for a chat."

"Oh, and another thing else, Mr. Marx. This has nothing to do with Peg, but I wanted to thank you," the young woman said. "Your brother did . . . well, not Zeppo himself, but someone from his talent agency. They called me last night and said they thought they might be able to place me in a small little part over at RKO."

"That's splendid, Sally," said Groucho.

"So . . . well, I'm sorry I thought you were just conning me the other day."

"Why do you think it says 'In Groucho We Trust' on all the coins, my child? You've got to have faith. Good luck." He hung up, put the cap back on the fountain pen and stood. "Could be we're getting closer to some answers."

Twenty

I still didn't have my shoes on when somebody started pounding on the front door of Jane's cottage.

"Open in the name of the law," shouted someone in a hardly convincing Irish brogue. "Faith and begonias, 'tis no good you're up to in there, to be sure."

"Groucho?" said Jane, setting down her fork.

"Groucho." I was already up from the table, heading for the doorway of the breakfast nook.

"Bejabbers," Groucho was calling out. "If you don't open up soon, it'll be tear gas we'll be after using. Or you might prefer the bloodhounds. If you can wait till next week, we'll be having a special and you can get dogs *and* gas for the same low price as—"

"Come in," I invited, pulling the door open wide.

"Do you realize what your being found here will do to this poor child's reputation? Why, until you came into her life, she was as pure as the driven snow," Groucho said. "And if you've ever driven snow around for any length of time, you know how pure that can be."

Reaching out, I took hold of the sleeve of his checkered sport coat and tugged him across the threshold. "Having crazed comedians bellowing on her doorstep isn't going to do her reputation much good either."

The morning paper he'd had tucked up under his arm fell to the carpet as he came, a bit lopsidedly, inside. "Oh, I don't know. If I lived nearby, I'd be immensely impressed to notice America's best-loved jester cutting capers on my neighbor's stoop."

"We're not talking about W. C. Fields here."

"Youth can be so cruel." Groucho, squatting, retrieved his newspaper. "If you're finished insulting a poor broken old man, my boy, we'll get down to brass tacks," he said, straightening up. "And if you expect me to make some lowbrow remark about sitting on tacks—you're absolutely right. Wait now, while I dredge up something apt."

"Good morning, Groucho." Jane was standing near the kitchen doorway, eying him.

"Top of the morning to you, colleen."

"Would you care to join us for breakfast?"

He studied the ceiling for a few seconds, considering the invitation. "Well, I'd be delighted—if you could provide something like cinnamon toast."

"How about cinnamon toast?"

"Close enough. I'm yours."

Jane gave him a very brief smile and stepped into the kitchen.

Groucho proceeded to unfold the paper. "Perhaps you've been wondering, between bouts of lust, whatever happened to that dead chap we bumped into in the hothouse yesterday."

I frowned. "Damn, I forgot all about him. I guess because of all the other stuff that happened subsequently."

"Yes, a blow on the bean can do serious damage to the thinking process and the memory." He turned to an inner page of the first section. "Once, some years ago, I was strolling along Cahuenga Boulevard—I had, mind you, no earthly business on Cahuenga Boulevard. It was simply that I loved the sound of it. When friends would inquire where I'd been, I reveled in responding, 'Oh, just strolling along Cahuenga Boulevard.' It often struck them dumb with awe and envy to hear me pronounce Cahuenga Boulevard so trippingly. Those who were already pretty dumb, it made dizzy and gave prickly heat. At any rate, while strolling along Cahuenga Boulevard on this particular fateful day, a safe dropped out of an upper-story office building window and smacked me square on the noggin. Well, sir, I have to tell you—I couldn't remember a darn thing for days on end. And for about a week after that, even when I wasn't on my end. Among the things I couldn't remember were the capital of North Dakota, the boiling point of borscht, the middle name of the first girl who ever kissed me in the ear, the capital of South Dakota and—"

"Am I wrong in assuming there was something in this paper you wanted to show me?"

"Well, of course, Rollo. You don't think I came all the way to this shanty merely to eat toast and deliver sentimental recitations on the cognitive processes." He folded the page in half and pointed to a small story just below the fold. "I found this item while reading the morning paper."

The headline said FORMER STUDIO TECHNICIAN FOUND SHOT and the subhead added *Body Discovered In Canyon.* It seems the body of Arnold Siegel, 46, had been discovered the night before in a stretch of woodlands up in Coldwater Canyon. He'd been shot twice in the back, then dumped there. Unemployed in recent months, Siegel had worked as an electrician for both Paramount and Monarch. The police had no immediate leads, but hinted at a gangland tie-in.

When I'd finished reading the story, I said, "Siegel has to be the same one."

"Since nobody's mentioned finding a similar corpse on Warren Stander's premises, I'm betting it is, sure."

"How'd Siegel get from Bel Air to Coldwater Canyon?"

Taking his paper back, Groucho folded it to its original shape and then tossed it on the sofa. "The most likely explanation is that, as we both believe, some of Vince Salermo's torpedoes took care of Siegel to keep him from peppering us," he said, locking his hands behind his back and crouching slightly. "After you and I rushed off to wow the masses with a snappy rendition of your script, these goons slipped in and carted the corpse off."

"Seems logical."

"Or possibly, though I doubt it, Stander found the remains of Arnie Siegel and had some of the servants take the body out and dump it. Having to explain a corpse in your hothouse can be embarrassing for a high-placed broadcast executive."

"Unlikely," I said. "Now we'd better find out who hired Siegel."

"Exactly," said Groucho. "I've got another lead to follow up, which I'll tell you about in a minute, so can you handle that?"

"Sure, yeah," I answered. "I know a couple of reliable informants who specialize in information about the shady side of the movie business."

"There's another side?"

"And if that doesn't turn up anything, I'll track down Siegel's next of kin."

Jane emerged from the kitchen carrying a platter. "Toast is on."

"You'll forgive me if I eat and run," said Groucho as he followed her to the breakfast room. "But I really think the game is afoot. In fact, by now it's probably grown to two or three feet at least."

Twenty-one

The Young Actresses' Club was on a side street off Cherokee in Hollywood. It was a three-story imitation adobe building with slanting red tile roofs. To get to the lobby you had to cross a small walled-in courtyard that had a goldfish pond at its center and a half dozen bedraggled palm trees circling its fringes.

When Groucho, as I found out later, came striding purposefully across the bright morning courtyard, there was a fat calico cat sprawled beside the little pool, patiently watching the flickering fish.

"You'd make a great movie mogul," Groucho mentioned to the cat as he pushed the lobby door open. "Or maybe an agent."

The lobby was cool and shadowy. On one of the three fat sofas two pretty young actresses were sitting, sharing a copy of a movie script.

"I bet it is him," whispered the blonde as Groucho drew near.

"No, it's not," said the redhead.

"It is."

"No, because he has a moustache."

Groucho had walked on past by this time. Slowing, he came to a full stop, pivoted and went back over to them. "It is me," he confided. "But I left the moustache in the car."

"Oh, we're sorry, Mr. Marx," apologized the redhead. "We weren't meaning to be rude."

"That's a pity. Rudeness is a quality more young people ought to cultivate." He bowed to each of them in turn and aimed again for the desk.

"I told you it was him," whispered the blonde.

A heavyset woman in a flowered dress was sitting at the switchboard, smoking a homemade cigarette and reading last month's issue of *Dime Detective.* "Why, it's Groucho Marx," she said, looking up and chuckling, "as I live and breathe."

"I'm glad you confirmed that you are living and breathing," Groucho told her. "Because when I first got a squint at you, I really wasn't sure. 'What are they doing with that stuffed hootchy-kootchy dancer in their lobby?'" I asked of myself."

"Oh, you're such a silly person, Mr. Marx."

"I know, and that's why they threw me out of the seminary," he said, resting an elbow on the desk. "Now then, my dear lady, perhaps you can help me. I'd like to have a brief chat with Hulda Bjornsen if it can be arranged."

Frowning, the woman snuffed out her cigarette in an abalone shell ashtray. "It's the funniest thing, Mr. Marx, but she didn't come in today," she said, shaking her head. "Hulda is just about the most reliable maid we have on the hotel staff.

Even though she doesn't own a telephone, if she's not going to be in to work, why, she makes sure to phone us from a neighbor's. And, the fact is, she hardly ever misses a day at all."

"But you say Hulda didn't show up today—and she hasn't phoned?"

"That's it, yes, Mr. Marx. I'm been worrying if I oughtn't to—"

"Where does she live?"

"Down in Venice, in a little house near one of those smelly old canals." She gestured in the direction of a filing cabinet. "I can get you her address, if you're thinking of running down there."

"That's precisely what I'm thinking of doing," Groucho said.

At a few minutes shy of noon, I was climbing up Bunker Hill in L.A. The steep cement steps ran more or less parallel to the Angel's Flight funicular railway and on my left a trolley car was bumping its way up the incline to Hill Street. I was heading for a boarding house halfway up the hill.

Tall palm trees dotted the climb, along with a large accumulation of shrubs. There were a couple of hotels on my side of the street, plus an assortment of once proud Victorian mansions, rich with spires and cupolas and intricate gingerbread, that now served as boarding houses and, in at least two instances, bordellos.

The informant I was going to see resided in a converted three-story Victorian that had, quite some time in the past, been painted lemon yellow and trimmed in chocolate brown. It had a wide porch, and sitting in a wicker rocker was a very fat woman of sixty-some years.

"Guess my age," she requested as I climbed the swayback wooden steps to the wide, sheltered porch.

"Under a hundred." I hit the top step and headed for the screen door.

"You must be Frank Denby."

I stopped. "I am, yeah."

"Tim's not back yet, but he said for you to wait," she said, nodding at a wicker armchair. "Would you like a glass of lemonade?"

"Not especially."

"I was going to suggest that if you did, you go in and tap on Mrs. Sheridan's door," she said. "We don't have an icebox ourselves, but she's got one and she's always brewing up pitchers of the stuff."

I ignored the wicker chair and perched on the ornately carved porch railing. "You're Mrs. O'Hearn?"

"I'm Tim's common-law wife actually."

"There's no need to tell people your goddamn life story, Agnes." A thin, pale man of about fifty came up the steps, carrying a quart bottle of Regal Pale Beer and a head of wilted lettuce in a green string bag. "Sorry I'm late, Frank."

"We've been having a perfectly nice conversation," she said.

O'Hearn grunted and pushed the screen door open. "Come on up to my room and we'll talk," he invited.

The dim hall of the venerable boarding house smelled of last night's dinner, and O'Hearn's dim apartment smelled of stale beer, dead cigarettes and spoiled food. A partially eaten cheese sandwich, fuzzed with greenish mold, rested in a cracked saucer atop the tangle of dirty underwear piled on the unmade bed. Another remnant of sandwich, thick with a white fuzzy growth, sat in an empty cigar box amid a scatter of mismatched shoes against the wall.

Spread out on the floor were a dozen recent racing tip sheets, each one annotated in the margins in O'Hearn's jittery scrawl.

"Be careful who you shack up with." My informant seated himself in a lopsided armchair, not bothering to move the pile of movie trade papers piled on the faded cushion. "Agnes is a lousy housekeeper."

I sat gingerly on the edge of a relatively uncluttered straight-back chair. "What've you found out for me, Tim?"

He made a just-a-minute gesture with his left hand. He carefully placed the string bag on the floor beside his chair, reached in and pulled out the quart of beer. "Just let me find a church key and then I'll report."

He got up, wandered over to a small rolltop desk in the corner and rummaged around through the mix of newspapers, tip sheets, file folders and empty cigarette packs until he unearthed a bottle opener.

After opening the brown bottle, taking a drink and settling into the chair again, O'Hearn said, "Things are different these days than they were back when you were working for the *Times,* Frank. The depression has lessened, wages are going up again, people are—"

"How much for the information?"

"Ten bucks."

"Five."

"Hey, I was out in the hot sun for over two damn hours working on this," he pointed out. "Eight."

"Six."

"Make it seven-fifty or we don't have a deal."

"Okay. What did you get?"

He drank more of the beer. "Arnold Siegel hasn't worked for any of the studios for over a year," he began. "A fondness for booze and a bad temper did the poor bastard in."

"That takes care of whom he hasn't been working for."

"Hold your horses," O'Hearn said. "Most recently, from what I've been able to dig up so far, Siegel's been doing odd jobs for Justin LaSalle."

"LaSalle, huh? What sort of odd jobs?"

"Donkey work mostly. Pick up a piece of antique furniture at an auction house, deliver it to a client of LaSalle's. Heavy lifting, truck driving, stuff of that nature."

I rubbed a knuckle across my nostrils. "Anything to connect Siegel with the Monarch or Paragon studios?"

"I can't link up Siegel directly," replied my informant. "But I can tie in LaSalle."

"How?"

"LaSalle's been doing a big redecorating job for Jack Gardella, the Monarch troubleshooter. Gardella just bought a beach house in Malibu and that swish is fixing it up for him."

"Gardella," I said, mostly to myself. May Sankowitz's cowpoke had spotted Peg having dinner with Gardella not that long ago.

O'Hearn wiped beer foam from his lips with the back of his hand. "Want me to keep digging, Frank?"

"Yeah, at least another five dollars worth."

"I'll give you something right now for free."

"What?"

"Gardella is a mean son of a bitch," he told me. "You really don't want to mess with the guy."

"So I keep hearing," I said and stood up.

Twenty-two

Like its namesake in Italy, the beach town of Venice, California, has canals, a series of them running from the Pacific and bringing in sea water. Each of the canals is about ten feet deep and something like fourteen feet wide. Small narrow concrete bridges arch over them.

Back in the 1920s the town was supposedly quaint and colorful, but now, a decade and more later, there's a run-down feel to it, especially in the part that tried to recapture the charm of the original Venice. The water in the canals has a brownish scum on it and garbage, including beer bottles and an occasional dead cat, can be seen floating in it. The odors of brine and decay are strong in the air.

"This spa's really in need of a plumber," commented Groucho to himself as he drove across another of the small, curved bridges. He crossed one more bridge and spotted Napoli Canal. Driving over a third bridge, he turned onto the street that ran along behind the small stucco houses that faced the stagnant canal.

As he pulled up and parked behind Hulda Bjornsen's little house, two sooty seagulls came fluttering down through the midday sky to light on the dusty red tiles of the roof.

The impact of their landing dislodged one of the curved tiles. It broke free, came plummeting down to the weedy back lawn. Surprised, both gulls gave complaining squawks and then flapped away.

"There's a moral there somewhere." Groucho stood for a few seconds watching the birds fly off toward the ocean.

The flagstone path leading to the back door was muddy, each stone making a squishy sound as he stepped on it. When he pushed the buzzer beside the wooden door, a metallic rasp-berry sound echoed inside the place. Nobody responded.

Groucho took a cigar out of his coat pocket, unwrapped it and poked the buzzer again.

Still no answer.

But he became aware of a faint thumping noise inside the maid's little house. "Hulda?" he called, cupping his hands. "Are you in there?"

He heard the thumping again.

Groucho tried the door handle and discovered that the back door wasn't locked. Hunching some, he opened the door and shoved it slowly inward. "Hulda?"

The thumping was repeated, from the front of the house.

He entered the shadowy corridor that ran from back door to front. As he passed the kitchen, Groucho noticed that it had been ransacked and that dishes, silverware and newspapers were scattered across the yellow linoleum floor. "Damn, they beat me to it," he muttered.

The living room was equally disrupted, with books and magazines tossed hither and yon, a lamp on its side and the chair cushions slashed and their innards spilled. From a closet came three more thumps.

Carefully, crouched, he moved through the debris and took hold of the handle.

Inside, gagged with a towel and tied with lengths of white clothesline, was a thin blond woman in a blue terrycloth robe. She made a murmuring sound when she saw Groucho looking over her.

"I'm pleased to see you're still alive," Groucho told her as he reached in and, grunting some, hefted her out of the closet.

He tripped over a spilled box of chocolates, skidded on a fallen copy of the *Saturday Evening Post* and dropped her atop the disemboweled sofa.

"Relax, Hulda—well, actually, I suppose there's not much else you can do at the moment." He fished a pocketknife out of his jacket, opened it and started cutting the ropes.

The maid muttered against the gag.

"Oops, should've taken care of that thing first." Shutting the knife, Groucho unfastened the gag.

Hulda coughed, cleared her throat, made spitting motions with her lips. "Thank you, Mr. Marx," she said. "I suppose you came by for the same reason they did."

"Not to tie you up and dump you in a closet, no," he said, returning to cutting the clothesline. 'But I am interested in the pictures Peg McMorrow gave you to take care of for her."

"Pictures? What makes you think it was—"

"Wasn't it photos?"

Hulda swallowed, allowing him to help her achieve a sitting

position on what was left of her sofa. "Well, I think so, yes, Mr. Marx," she answered.

"They got them?"

"Oh, yes," she said, nodding. "They only had to slap me once and I took them right to where I'd hidden the packet. I had it fastened to the underside of a bureau drawer in my bedroom. Used bandage tape."

"You gave them the pictures, but they tossed your house anyway?"

"They wanted to make sure, they told me, I wasn't holding back anything."

"When were they here?"

"Early this morning, just as the sun was coming up." The last of the ropes fell away. "I was in the kitchen fixing myself a poached egg, when they came busting in."

Groucho crouched, helping her rub at her arms. "How many louts and what did they look like?"

"Two of them," answered Hulda. "One was a big fellow, blond, with his hair cut real short. What they call a heinie haircut, you know. The other one was smaller, about your size but very well dressed. Slicked hair, parted in the middle, little squiggly moustache."

"Any idea who they were?"

She hesitated. "I don't know them and they didn't drop any hints while they were taking the packet and tying me up," she said.

"But maybe you saw them before?"

"The smaller one," she said finally. "I may've seen him a couple days ago. I think he's the same man who came into the Young Actresses' Club and asked for somebody at the desk."

"Know who he was asking after?"

Hulda shook her head. "I was vacuuming the rugs and I couldn't hear a darn thing, Mr. Marx."

"Did they tell you, either one of them, how they knew you had the pictures?"

"No, but they seemed very certain that I did."

"Might've been a bluff that they've been trying on all Peg's friends," he said thoughtfully.

"It's very lucky for me you got here when you did, Mr. Marx. I live alone, you know, and I could've stayed in that darn closet all day."

He righted a straightback chair that had been knocked over and sat, gingerly, on its slashed seat. "I'll call your doctor for you, Hulda."

"No, that's okay. I'm all right and I can't afford to pay for a visit just now."

"I'll take care of that if—"

"No, no thanks, Mr. Marx. I'll just clean up a little here and then get into the hotel. They must be wondering where the—"

"Take the day off," he suggested. "I'll phone the hotel and explain that you're under the weather."

"That would be nice, although I hate to miss—"

"I can also make up what you'd be earning today," he said, reaching for his wallet.

"No, I couldn't let you do—"

"Sure, you can." He took out a five-dollar bill and handed it to the maid.

"That's too much."

"Now perhaps," said Groucho, ignoring her attempts to return the money, "you could answer a few questions for me."

Hulda folded the five and slipped it into the pocket of her robe. "If I can, Mr. Marx, yes, of course."

"You saw Peg for dinner a few nights ago."

"Yes, the poor kid."

"Okay, what did she say about this packet of pictures?"

Hulda leaned forward on the sofa, rubbing at her knee. "Well, in the first place, she never exactly said they were snapshots," she told him. "Only that she had something that was valuable to her, but that there'd been some burglaries in her neighborhood lately and she'd feel a lot safer if I kept this packet for her."

"What did she say was in the packet?"

Hulda shook her head. "Only that it was something valuable and that I should hide it in a safe place."

"For how long?"

"Beg pardon?"

"Was Peg planning to come and get it back later on?"

"Oh, I see what you mean, Mr. Marx," Hulda said. "Well, I got the idea, though she never said it directly, that this wasn't a long-term thing. That she'd be taking the packet back in a week or so."

"What about her career? Did she tell you about signing a contract with one of the studios?"

"She did, Mr. Marx," Hulda replied. "And it was the oddest thing, because I hear the girls talking around the hotel and I have a conversation with one or another of them sometimes. Anyway, the rumor I'd been hearing was that Peg was about set to sign with Paragon. I thought that sounded wonderful and when, out of the blue, she invited me to dinner, why, I congratulated her."

"But she said it wasn't Paragon?"

Hulda blinked. "Yes, exactly. It was funny. She laughed, but it was—well, I always liked Peg a lot—but this was a nasty laugh. I didn't like the sound of it at all. She said she was going to be a star at Monarch."

"She tell you why?"

"I asked her, but all she'd say was that Eli Kurtzman and his toadies had finally realized her true worth. Something like that."

Groucho stood up. "What about the pictures, Hulda?"

"I never, honestly, opened the packet to look at them."

"But you knew there were snapshots in there."

"Well, I was curious. She reached into her purse and slipped out this little package wrapped in green paper, slid it across the table and told me to slip it into my purse in a hurry," Hulda said. "When I got home here, well, I felt the package, held it up to the light. It was snapshots, I'm near certain, about six or seven of them."

Groucho said, "You sure you're going to be all right, Hulda?"

"Fine, I'm fine."

"Then I'll be up and doing," he announced.

"Thank you for helping me, Mr. Marx," she said. "And good luck on your new radio show."

"The radio show," said Groucho as he moved for the doorway. "Gad, I'd nearly forgotten about that."

Twenty-three

Groucho leaned closer to the microphone and said, "And just what makes you think your husband is dead, Mrs. Uppercase?"

"Well, you can see for yourself, Mr. Transom. Just look at how he's lying there in front of the fireplace."

"Ah, so that's your husband, is it? I thought it was a bearskin rug."

"Poor Rowland was a bit shaggy, but that's his still and lifeless form."

"I was wondering why a grizzly bear would be wearing a houndstooth suit."

"Can you solve—"

"Of course, there have been times when I wondered why a hound would be wearing a bearskin cap. And once I even wondered where elephants go to die. But then I was invited to an elephant's funeral and that settled that."

"Try to curb your silliness, Mr. Transom."

"And you try to curb that spaniel of yours, Mrs. Uppercase. Everybody in the neighborhood is complaining about—"

"Are you sure that you're even a detective?"

"Of course I'm a detective. If you'd like, I can show you my diploma. Or better yet—I can show you the scar from my operation. That's in a more interesting place. Although, come to think of it, the diploma's in an interesting place, too. That is, if you consider Cleveland, Ohio, an interesting place. But as for me—"

"Please, Mr. Transom, please. What am I to do about my poor departed husband?"

"Well, the first thing I'd do is throw a blanket over him. Frankly, I'm getting tired of looking at the fellow."

"No, I mean—"

"And while you're at it, if you have an extra blanket, toss one over yourself, Mrs. Uppercase. You're no sight for sore eyes yourself, you know. In fact, if I owned a site like you, I'd build a parking lot on it."

"Mr. Transom, ace detective or no ace detective, I don't intend to pay you twenty dollars a day, plus expenses, to be insulted."

"No, for insults this good the fee is fifty bucks."

"It seems to me that if you were any sort of detective— you'd start asking questions."

"You're absolutely right. So here's a question—When do we eat?"

"No, I mean questions about my poor husband."

"Well, it's no use asking when he's going to eat, is it?"

"Mr. Transom, you are—"

"Being dead will take your appetite right away. Anybody who really wants to lose weight should seriously consider dropping dead. And perhaps that was your husband's motive, Mrs.

Uppercase, because he does look a bit on the pudgy side. Or maybe it's just the suit. But then, who'd buy a pudgy suit?"

From inside the glass booth, the director said, "That's sounding great, Groucho. We'll take our break here and come back to the rehearsal in about an hour."

Groucho dropped his script to the studio floor, hopped to the left and put both arms around Margaret Dumont, whom we'd been able to land for the part of Mrs. Uppercase. "Maggie, my pet, you are another Bernhardt, another Bankhead, another Constance Collier." He kissed her on the cheek with a loud smack. "It's only too bad nobody is in the market for another one of any of those ladies."

She smiled politely and disengaged herself from his grip. "You stepped on one of my lines, Groucho. Please, don't do that on the night of the actual broadcast."

"It's only because, when I'm in your radiant presence, I get all flustered and—oh, gorsh." He dug his toe into the carpeted floor and rolled his eyes.

"You were sensational, Groucho," said Junior Orem over the mike in the booth. "If I'm any judge, this show is going to be a smash hit."

"If you were any judge, you wouldn't be passing off South American cathouse floor sweepings as coffee," said Groucho, unwrapping a cigar.

"You're a great little kidder, Groucho," said our sponsor, beaming down at Groucho through the slanted glass window of the control room.

"Let this be a lesson to you, Rollo," said Groucho, picking up the script again and joining me down in the front row of seats. "Once you establish yourself as a comedian, you can thereafter tell every fool and nitwit on the face of the earth the unvarnished truth about themselves and they'll laugh and take it as a joke."

"That wasn't the truth you told, Orem," I mentioned. "If Orem Brothers Coffee was made from whorehouse sweepings, it'd taste a lot better than it does."

"Well, perhaps, but the great insight into life I've just imparted still holds true," he said, chomping on the end of the cigar but not lighting it. "Speaking of seamy romance, are you rushing right over to Jane's crib after this rehearsal?"

"Nope, her boss is still sick and she's got to turn out a *Hillbilly Willie* Sunday page by tomorrow," I answered. "I won't be seeing her at all tonight."

"Ah, the old I-have-to-draw-for-the-funny-papers excuse," he said, leaning back in the seat. "You'd think a woman of her evident intelligence would be able to come up with a better one than that. I bet she and Rod Tommerlin are, even as we speak, rolling in the hay and exchanging fevered words of . . . what's wrong, Rollo?"

My expression must've indicated that I wasn't amused. "Nothing, Groucho," I said. "It's only . . ." I shrugged.

"You're not jealous of that dispenser of cornpone, are you?"

"Not really, but I think he has made a few passes at Jane and that annoys me."

"Tommerlin makes passes at all women from the age of fifteen upwards," he explained. "Make that fourteen and up. He's notorious for his amorous lunges and there's been a campaign initiated to put saltpeter in his food or possibly get him a leash. Don't worry about Jane, she's not going to succumb to a putz like Tommerlin."

"I suppose not."

"We seem to have settled your lovelorn problems for the nonce," said Groucho. "If we locate Justin LaSalle, we can settle them for the nance. Let us go then, you and I, and get a bite to eat. We can discuss what progress we've made today on the case and plan our strategy." He stood up, stretched and then waved at Margaret Dumont, who was sitting up near one of the microphones making notes in the margin of her script. "I won't be able to meet you in your dressing room as planned, Maggie. But we're still on for the dog races later in the evening." He tugged me up out of my seat. "Let's be out and about, Rollo."

Twenty-four

The rehearsal ended at a few minutes after ten and at ten-thirty, after traveling a circuitous zigzagging route through Hollywood, I was parking my coupe on a side street off Sunset. The night was windy and the leaves of the pepper trees overhead were rattling and sighing.

Groucho twisted around in the passenger seat so that he could scan the night street behind us. "Well, there's still no sign of anybody tailing us, thugs, goons, assassins or what have you," he concluded after a moment. "We've succeeded in eluding all of our potential pursuers. And, Rollo, it's not easy to be sly and unobtrusive when you're tooling round in a vehicle that's the color of a lemon with jaundice."

"You were a mite vague at dinner," I reminded him. "Explain to me again why we're dropping in on this particular photographer."

Groucho found a cigar in his coat pocket. "I got to thinking—something I try to do at least once a week—about snapshots and photos. Now then, if you shoot a roll of film of your dear old grandmother—do you have a grandmother, by the way?"

"Nope."

"Well, you shoot a roll of some photogenic relative or other cavorting at the beach or standing on the front lawn and squinting into the lens. That presents no problem, since you can openly pop into the nearest Thrifty Drugstore or the corner camera shop and have it developed without fear. Nothing wrong with snapping pictures of some doddering old coot with sand in his shoes."

"I see, yeah. You can't do that with a batch of supposedly incriminating photos, especially if they happen to show people in the sack together."

"When I knew Peg, she told me that she'd now and then snap some somewhat steamy pics of some of her lady friends and their beaus," he continued.

"But nothing steamy of you?"

"Rollo, in all my long and varied career as a mangy lover, I've never been dimwitted enough to let anybody get a shot of me in dishabille," he assured me. "As I was saying before the heckling commenced—while I was driving home from scenic Venice this afternoon, I recalled that Peg always had Eddie Sutterford develop those special rolls of film for her."

"He's the guy who took those publicity shots of her, isn't he?"

"The same. Eddie specializes in publicity stuff, plus some glamour photography and cheesecake of varying degrees of respectability." Groucho unwrapped the cigar. "It occurred to me that if Peg had some pictures that she couldn't trust to a regular developing outfit—why, she'd probably go to Eddie. He'd done similar stuff for her before, he liked her and she could trust him."

"He might not, even if he did do the job, admit it."

"Oh, I know a few things about Eddie's shady past that'll probably prompt him to confide in us." Thrusting the cigar between his teeth and then glancing carefully around, he stepped out of the car and into the windy night.

The lights were on at Eddie Sutterford's photography studio, which occupied a shingle cottage sitting up on the crest of a grassy lot on Sunset Boulevard. The close-cropped lawn had several small billboards, each about the size of an upended Ping-Pong table, dotting it. Floodlights illuminated huge portrait photos of movie actresses.

"Reminds one of Easter Island," observed Groucho. "Except the heads there are not nearly so cute."

Walking up the twisting gravel path to the photographer's front door, we passed giant photos of Ginger Rogers, Alice Faye, Joan Bennett and Barbara Stanwyck.

Groucho tapped his cigar with his forefinger, and ashes and sparks went scattering away on the night wind. "Zeppo is Stanwyck's agent," he mentioned as we approached the porch. "He also manages the venerable Evelyn Venable. I mention that fact solely because I do so enjoy saying Evelyn Venable aloud."

"I'll write it into the next script."

"By the way, I didn't actually step on any of Maggie Dumont's lines at the damned rehearsal," he said, puffing on the cigar. "The dear lady is getting along in years and has become increasingly grumpy and just a teeny-weeny bit paranoid."

"Groucho, she's exactly the same age as you are."

He'd been reaching for the brass knocker, but instead he stopped still and rose up on his toes. "I find that unbelievable, Rollo," he told me, settling down on his heels. "Yet I suppose it must be her dissolute life style that has caused her to age so incredibly, whereas my own sedate mode of existence, which your average choirboy would find dull, accounts for the glow of youth I exude."

I reached around him and whacked the knocker, which was in the shape of a tiny bulldog head, several times against its brass plate.

That produced no immediate results.

After taking another deep puff of his cigar, Groucho whapped the upper panel of the door with his fist. "Open up, Sutterford! We've had a complaint that you're photographing totally naked fat ladies in there."

"In a minute, Groucho," called a reedy voice. "Hold on, huh?"

"At least nobody seems to have tied him up and dumped him in a closet," said Groucho. "Although, considering Eddie's sexual proclivities, he'd probably rather enjoy that."

The wind hit at the door just as the photographer opened it. The door went flapping back into him.

Groucho jumped across the threshold, pulling me in after him. With his help, Sutterford got the door shut again.

He was a plump man, about five foot six and almost bald. His skin, which was dotted with perspiration, was a bluish white in color and he smelled faintly of chemicals. "Always a great kick to see you, Groucho," Sutterford assured him. He stayed put in the hallway.

"I know, Eddie. I can tell by the festive mood my advent seems to have put you in." Groucho exhaled smoke. "This is my associate, Frank Denby."

"Pleased to meet you." He didn't extend his hand. "The situation here is this, Groucho. I'm in the middle of a shoot and—"

"Gad, sir, don't tell me you actually do have a naked fat lady on the premises?"

"Nothing like that," he said. "It's only a young starlet who wants some cheesecake shots for her portfolio."

"How young?" Groucho's eyebrows climbed slightly.

"She's of age, don't worry," said Sutterford, glancing at a closed door across the hall. "The thing is, Groucho, she's shy about having strangers watching when—"

"I'm noted for my ability to become almost sickeningly friendly with just about any female in under three minutes, Eddie," Groucho told him. "So introduce us and this little girl and I will be jolly chums in nothing flat."

"She's not a child, but—"

"Tell you what." Groucho took hold of the photographer's coat sleeve just above the elbow. "Let's move from blarney to the real purpose of this visit. I actually dropped by, knowing that you usually work late in this sinkhole, to talk to you about something other than what goes on in your studio between you and undraped maidens."

Sutterford pulled free of Groucho's grip and took a few steps back along the corridor. "What did you want to talk to me about?"

Groucho slouched closer to him. "Peg McMorrow."

The photographer glanced again at the closed door. "This isn't a good time."

"On the contrary, it's an ideal time," contradicted Groucho. "Otherwise I might drop in elsewhere and talk about other topics. Such as, for example, the part you played in that picture-taking session down in Malibu only last—"

"Okay, all right, Groucho," he said. "Let me go in and tell her to take a break. Then we can go into my office and talk." He nodded at me, adding, "Groucho isn't always that amiable a guy, you know."

"That's a surprise to me," I said.

Twenty-five

Resting both elbows on the desk, Groucho leaned closer to the uneasy photographer. "Baloney," he accused.

On Sutterford's side of the small, uncluttered desk his swivel chair creaked as he leaned back, avoiding Groucho's accusing gaze. "You have my word," he said in his piping voice. "I haven't developed any photos for Peg in over a year. Honestly." He sighed. "I hadn't even seen the poor girl in months."

"If they make an official search of this pest spot, Eddie, complete with warrants and fire axes," Groucho pointed out, "they'll probably find a hell of a lot more than just the copies of Peg's photos that you kept for yourself."

"What makes you think I kept any?"

"Because I know you, know how you work and how you think." Groucho leaned closer.

The photographer pulled back a few more inches, until the back of his chair bonked one of his filing cabinets. "Well, okay," he admitted. "Yeah, I did keep a set for myself."

Groucho said nothing.

After a few seconds Sutterford said, "But they're not what you think."

Sitting up and spreading his hands wide, Groucho said, "I have no preconceptions. We simply want to see the damn prints."

"There are only five shots," he said.

"That's all she took?" I asked.

The bald photographer nodded, looking from me to Groucho. "You guys want to see them, though, huh?"

"Better than that," said Groucho. "I want you to hand them over to me and then forget you ever had them."

Very slowly, Sutterford got up. "You don't believe she killed herself, do you?"

"I don't, no."

The photographer shuffled across his small office to another filing cabinet. He knelt, breathing heavily, and tugged out the bottom drawer. He bent further, sliding one hand under the drawer and pulling at something that was apparently attached there. "I hid them here," he explained as he pulled out a manila envelope with pieces of tape dangling from it.

"A cunning hiding place," remarked Groucho.

Sutterford was perspiring more profusely when he stood up. "They're really nothing special," he said, handing the envelope over to Groucho. "You'll see."

"If they're nothing special, why'd you stash them in a secret hiding place?"

"I didn't do that until after I heard Peg was dead."

"You figured these pictures had something to do with her death?"

"I didn't figure anything, Groucho. I just felt uneasy—you know? Had a hunch I didn't want anybody to come across this stuff."

I left my chair as Groucho took the snapshots out of the envelope and spread them out on his side of the desktop. "This is it?" he asked, disappointed.

The snaps had been enlarged twice up. All five had the same location and showed a man and a woman, fully clothed, in a woodland setting. They were facing each other and appeared to be arguing. In the background you could make out a lake with a scattering of rustic cabins on its far side. All of the pictures looked to have been shot in a relatively short span of time. And it seemed obvious that the couple didn't know they were being photographed.

Groucho tapped his forefinger on one of the images of the handsome blond man. "This is Tom Kerry, isn't it? The second-rate swashbuckler at Monarch."

"It's Tom Kerry sure enough," I agreed. "But he's the top actor at the studio. And his upcoming epic, *The Pirate Prince,* is supposed to be a guaranteed box office smash."

"Where'd you hear that?"

"Johnny Whistler said it on his morning broadcast."

"Then it must be God's truth."

I picked up one of the pictures, nodded over at Sutterford. "Know who this woman is?"

"No idea. Never saw her before."

"Funny, I thought you might."

Groucho looked up at me. "I don't know her either. Is she in the movie business?"

The woman who was arguing with the movie star was a

slim, dark-haired woman of about forty. "Only peripherally. Her name's Babs McLaughlin," I said. "She's married to Benton McLaughlin, a writer over at MGM. I met her a couple years back when I covered a burglary for the *Times* that they'd had at their Pacific Palisades place."

"My God, are you a reporter?" asked Sutterford.

"Not anymore. Relax."

Groucho took back the picture I was holding, gathered up the other four and shuffled them absently together. "Why did Peg bring these to you, Eddie?" he asked. "You could take stuff like this to the corner drugstore and not raise an eyebrow."

Sutterford coughed into his hand. "Peg said she didn't want anybody to know about these pictures."

"Why?"

"She didn't say, Groucho."

"You sure?"

"Hey, listen, you knew Peg. She wasn't especially confiding. Played it close to the vest."

"She didn't hint at anything?"

"Just that these were important and I was to develop them and keep quiet."

I asked him, "She picked them up herself when they were ready?"

He nodded. "Yeah, and she was alone."

Groucho dealt out the pictures again. "Recognize the spot where they were taken?"

"Some forest area," I said. "Could be anyplace. California, Oregon, Washington."

"Eddie?"

"Same here. I don't know where they were shot and Peg never mentioned."

"When did she bring them in for you to develop?"

"Three weeks ago Monday."

Groucho collected the pictures into a handful, slid them back into the envelope and thrust the envelope into his breast pocket. "We'll have to discuss the possibilities implied in these images," he said to me.

"Do you mind if I get back to my starlet?" Sutterford was making his way toward the door.

Groucho said, "Go ahead, you don't want to keep these lasses up too late on a school night, Eddie. Oh, and don't mention that I've taken possession of these pictures."

"You think I'm nuts?" He hurried out of the office.

Twenty-six

There was a cop waiting for me in my living room when I got home that night at a little after ten P.M. I let myself in and there he was, a tall, thin man, wearing a tan overcoat and a blue suit. His gray fedora rested on one sharp knee and he was seated in an armchair under one of my inherited floor lamps reading my rough draft of the second *Groucho Marx, Master Detective* script.

"You want to finish reading that," I inquired, shutting the door behind me, "before you explain who the hell you are?"

"Branner," he said, closing the script and tossing it back on my coffee table. "Sort of funny, your script."

"You'd be Sergeant Branner of the Bayside police?"

He nodded. "Cold in your place."

"I hadn't noticed," I said. "Would you have anything like a warrant?"

"Not necessary on a friendly little visit like this, Denby."

"Most of my friends wait until I'm home before dropping in."

"Mind if I smoke?" he asked, lighting a Camel cigarette.

157

"Why exactly are you here, Sergeant?"

He inhaled the smoke deep inside him, then gave me a sympathetic look. It was the sort of look your doctor might give you just before informing you that you're dying of an incurable disease. "You're interested in Peg McMorrow," he told me.

Coming farther into my living room, I asked, "Yeah, so?"

"Don't be."

"What are you saying? You're telling me to stop looking into the death?"

"How could I do anything like that, Denby?" He dragged deeply on the Camel. "This is a free country, isn't it? You can go poking your nose into anything you damn well please."

"You didn't break in here just to tell me that, Sergeant."

"Well, I did also want to mention that there have been a rash of assaults and break-ins in your particular neighborhood lately," the lean cop said. "We find that people, such as yourself, who live alone are being robbed and beaten. Sometimes beaten quite badly." He stood up. "It's something to think about."

"I suppose it is."

"And you might warn your girlfriend, Miss Danner, about this, too." He moved toward my front door. "She could get quite seriously hurt, if she's not careful and—"

"You son of a bitch!" I made a lunge toward him.

He jumped back, held out a warning hand. "You don't want to assault an officer, Denby," he said. "It wouldn't look good on your record."

"Get out, just get the hell out of here," I told him, fists clenching at my sides.

He gave me that sympathetic look again, added a pitying smile. Taking hold of the doorknob, he slowly turned it. "You might mention to that Jew friend of yours up in Beverly Hills that people can also get hurt even in ritzy mansions." He let himself out.

I stood there, absently staring out at the darkness that was pressing against the windows. For a moment I had trouble breathing and my teeth came close to chattering. "Maybe it is cold in here," I murmured.

Angry and uneasy, I left my place a few minutes after Sergeant Branner's visit and went walking along the beach. Hands in pockets, I tromped over the damp sand. My shoulders were hunched, my chin was tucked down and I was getting a splendid view of the clam holes and the driftwood.

"It's not that you haven't been threatened by cops before," I was telling myself aloud.

That had happened fairly often when I was working on the *L.A. Times.* In fact, my attitude toward certain officers of the law, in Bayside and other unsavory towns, had contributed to my leaving the newspaper.

"You shouldn't have let him threaten Jane," I said, kicking at a crabshell.

But Branner, the bastard, was right about that. Slugging him wouldn't have been an especially bright move.

"If he covered up Peg's murder," I reminded myself, "and Groucho and I can prove it, then we'll have Branner's ass in a sling."

Not as immediately gratifying as hitting him, but a lot more devastating to him and his career as a crooked cop.

I noticed that I'd been walking in the direction of Jane's cottage. It was about eleven, but the lights were still on in her living room and the spare room that she used as a studio.

"Might as well drop by."

We hadn't planned to get together that night, but I decided I wanted to make sure she was all right and that nobody had been around threatening her.

"And, hell, I just simply want to see her."

I was about a half block from her house when the front door flapped open. A tall, heavyset man came hurrying out, something large and flat tucked under his arm.

He went striding off along the sidewalk in the opposite direction, climbed into a dark blue Cadillac and drove away.

The front door of Jane's cottage had remained open.

"Something's wrong," I said, running up across the lawn.

Before I reached the lighted doorway, Jane appeared there. Her eyebrows did a Groucho climb when she noticed my approach. "I'm flattered," she told me as I hit the porch, "that you came over here on a dead run."

I paused, caught my breath. "Who the hell was that?" I gestured toward the place where the departed Cadillac had been parked.

"That was Rod."

"Rod Tommerlin?"

"That Rod, yes. Come on in." She smiled, turned and headed into her living room.

I followed, shutting the door. "What was he doing here?"

Jane came back to where I'd halted. Placing her hands on my shoulders, she looked me directly in the eye. "I work for him. He came by to pick up the *Hillbilly Willie* Sunday page I just finished ghosting for him. I am not having an affair with him. That is not to say that he wouldn't like to have an affair with me, but then, Rod being Rod, he'd like to have an affair with just about every female from here to the border. It's you I happen to be fond of at the moment, which probably indicates a lack of taste and discernment on my part, but there it is. Would you like a cup of hot chocolate?"

I leaned and kissed her on the cheek. "Fine, yeah," I said.

She let go. "Accompany me to the kitchen," she invited. "Why the late visit?"

"Love knows no boundaries."

She lifted a tin of cocoa off a kitchen shelf. "Possibly, Frank, but you look a lot more distraught than usual."

"I keep forgetting there are Celtic mystics on your family tree."

"So explain yourself, huh?"

While the milk was heating in a saucepan, I told her about the visit from Sergeant Branner.

After she'd mixed two cups of chocolate and we were back in the living room, Jane said, "I seem to be changing."

"How so?"

"Well, last night I probably would've advised, as I've been doing ever since you and Groucho embarked on this detective business, to take Branner's warning to heart."

"But you're not going to suggest again that we quit?"

"No, damn it." She set her cup down on the coffee table. "I don't like Branner's breaking into your house and ordering you around. Maybe Mussolini's goons can do that, and maybe Hitler's storm troopers. But this isn't a fascist country—not yet anyway. You have to stand up to bullies like Branner and tell him where he can stuff it."

"He's also threatening you," I reminded her.

"Listen, I figure if I can ward off Rod Tommerlin, I can handle a few local cops." Picking up her cup, she sipped the chocolate. "Are you staying the night?"

"The thought hadn't crossed my mind until you brought it up," I said, trying to look guileless. "But it's a fine idea."

"I hope," she said, "your radio dialogue is more believable than this."

Twenty-seven

Jane answered the bedside phone when it rang at a few minutes beyond eight the next morning. "Hello?" she said after reaching across me to pick up the receiver. "Oh, good morning, Groucho."

I yawned and sat up.

"Well, there is somebody here sprawled out in the bed beside me," she was saying. "Hold on a minute and I'll see if I can identify him."

I held out my hand for the phone.

She kept it. "Well, it does sort of look like Frank," she told Groucho. "Okay, I'll see if he's in any condition to talk to you."

I took the receiver. "Hello, Groucho."

"Let me give you a bit of cautionary advice that may someday save your life, especially if you happen to find yourself lost in the Himalayas," he said. "Actually, this advice is also good for the Catskills." He cleared his throat. "That woman you're cohabiting with is much too flippant. Trade her in for a nice lumbering dimbulb if you want to live a life of serene and—"

"I appreciate your calling me to pass along advice to the lovelorn," I told him. "Was there any other reason for—"

"Quite obviously her strain of flippancy is of the contagious sort. I'm afraid that I must inform you, young man, that you've caught a bad case of it," observed Groucho. "But, yes, you may rest assured that I have a redeeming social purpose in disturbing you in your little love nest, Rollo."

"Glad to hear that."

"I had a late visit from Chico, also known as the fun-loving Rover Boy, last night," he continued.

"Speaking of visits, Sergeant Branner of the—"

"We'll get to that in a jiffy," he said. "Or if all the jiffies are spoken for, we'll have to travel by huff. Now to the point. I showed Chico the four photos I retained from the batch we got from our photographer chum. I assume, by the way, you haven't lost the one you took or traded it to the natives for some of those bright colored beads you're so fond of?"

"I still have it, yes. What does Chico know about Tom Kerry and Babs McLaughlin?"

"Nothing about that swashbuckling hambone," said Groucho. "But Chico pointed out something that I, being a studious follower of the local yellow press, should have recalled reading. There were stories, albeit small ones stuck in the back pages, about Mrs. McLaughlin in the papers a few weeks back."

"What sort of stories?"

"She's missing."

"Missing?"

"According to the reports that I unearthed out of the bundle of old newspapers I keep in the garage, Babs McLaughlin drove alone down to a small hideaway house she and her husband own down in Baja near Ensenada."

"Are we talking about the same weekend we know she was with Tom Kerry?"

"Precisely." I could hear Groucho taking a puff of his cigar. "She was seen in Ensenada on that Friday evening. But after that she seems to have vanished, along with her car. There are no servants at the little place down there and nobody who has any idea where she got to. She simply never came back."

"Have there been any follow-up stories?"

"Both your alma mater, the *Times,* and Mr. Hearst's rag, had small items two days ago to the effect that Babs McLaughlin remains among the missing," he said. "And the law isn't even bothering to pretend that they know where she might be."

"She must've left Ensenada that Friday and driven somewhere to meet Kerry."

"That's my notion. And those pictures with him surely weren't taken anywhere near Baja," he said. "So what we have to find out is where that rendezvous took place *and* why in the hell Peg was anywhere nearby."

"I've met Benton McLaughlin," I reminded him. "I can try to contact him and see if he—"

"No, let's hold off on that," suggested Groucho. "I'm going to check with the few reliable people I know at MGM, where McLaughlin toils as a writer, and see if I can gather any information obliquely and subtly. I'll give you another call toward sundown. Now what about your run-in with the minions of the law?"

"One minion," I corrected and told him about Sergeant Branner's visit.

"We must be on the right trail," said Groucho when I'd finished. "Otherwise he wouldn't be threatening you."

"I'd be a lot happier if I knew where the trail is leading."

"Well, just keep in mind that if you have sufficient pluck and luck then you're bound to win and that if you keep your eye on the bluebird you'll discover that every cloud has a silver lining, except on Tuesdays when we close early." He hung up.

I know where that is," said Jane.

We were having breakfast and I had showed her the snapshot Peg McMorrow had taken of Tom Kerry and Babs McLaughlin arguing beside a woodland lake.

"Where?"

She held up the photo, pointing to the tiny images of cabins on the far shore of the lake. "These are part of Shadow Lodge. The cabins are to the left of the lodge itself," she explained. "The place is on Lake Sombra, which is up in Northern California about twenty miles or so from Lake Tahoe."

"Never heard of it."

She placed the photo on the checkered oilcloth. "Well, Shadow Lodge doesn't advertise, Frank," she said. "It's the sort of place you go when you don't want to be noticed."

"Exactly what Kerry would pick for spending a weekend with somebody else's wife." I retrieved the photo and took another look at it. "Wonder what they were squabbling about?"

"Maybe just a lovers' quarrel."

As I slid the snap into my shirt pocket, an unpleasant thought hit me. I kept it to myself, but my face apparently gave me away.

Jane said quietly, "You're probably also wondering how come I know about the place."

"No, what you did before we met isn't—" I stopped talking, took a deep breath. "That sounds pretty damn patronizing, doesn't it? Actually, yes, I am feeling jealous. Even though you were there, if you were there at all, long before we even knew each other."

"I *was* there. Nearly two years ago," she said. "And, no, it wasn't with Rod Tommerlin."

"I didn't think it was."

"I went there, and probably stayed in one of those cabins you can see in the picture, with a man who couldn't risk being seen openly with me," Jane told me. "My only excuse is that I was much dippier then than I am now. But, since you haven't much to compare it with, you may think I'm pretty thoroughly dippy right now."

Grinning, I reached across and took hold of her hand. "Why, missy, you're hardly dippy at all," I assured her. "And me and all the wranglers are right fond of you."

"You and Groucho," she said. "Making jokes about things that hurt you."

"Okay, and now I'll return to being the detached reporter I was trained to be," I said.

"Knowing where Peg was that weekend ought to help you," she said.

"Yeah, but it also brings up a lot more questions that have to be answered," I said.

Twenty-eight

The Garden of Allah is at the intersection of Sunset and Crescent Heights Boulevard and spreads across three-plus acres. Back around the time of the Great War it was the private estate of Alla Nazimova. By the end of the 1920s Nazimova was no longer a high-paid movie star and she sold the property to some people who converted her mansion into a hotel and built a couple of dozen bungalows around it. There's a swimming pool that's supposedly shaped like the Black Sea, a lot of trees and shrubbery and a good deal of red tile and cream-colored stucco. Nazimova herself still has a suite, rent free, in the main building.

On that particular bright, clear autumn afternoon Groucho was slouching along a flagstone path that led to the bungalow he sought. From behind a chest-high hedge came a hissing sound.

Groucho slowed, frowning in the direction of the noise. "Charlie, is that you skulking in the underbrush?"

Charles Butterworth rose up, wobbling some, until his head

was completely visible above the hedge top. The actor beckoned Groucho to come closer. "Groucho, dear fellow, I wonder if you could lend me a hand?"

"Plenty of black coffee is what you need," advised Groucho, stepping closer.

"Quite possibly, Groucho, but at the moment I need some help with Bob here."

Groucho went up on tiptoe to peer over the hedge. "Jesus, Charlie, is he dead?"

Sprawled face-up in a bright red wheelbarrow was Robert Benchley. He was wearing a pair of polka dot swimming trunks and a very large yellow terrycloth robe. His eyes were closed, his mouth open, and his arms hung limply over the sides of the barrow.

"Dead?" Butterworth blinked, glancing down at his friend. "I don't think so, Groucho. I certainly hope not. I'd feel foolish if it turned out I've been pushing a dead man around in this damn thing. What I'm trying to do is get him back to his bungalow—but the task has proved too formidable."

"I'm not dead, I'm only sleeping," announced Benchley, taking hold of both sides of the wheelbarrow, opening his eyes and attempting to sit up.

That effort caused the barrow to teeter, sway and then topple over to the right. Benchley was dumped out onto a patch of pale green grass. He remained there, apparently asleep again.

Groucho found a break in the hedge, pushed through and trotted over to the fallen actor. "Bob, sleeping on grass is the major cause of hoof and mouth disease. Especially if you happen to be sleeping with a cow." He took hold of Benchley under the armpits. "Come, my lad, let's be up and doing."

"He usually holds his liquor better than this," remarked Butterworth, watching as Groucho succeeded in tugging Benchley up into a sitting position.

Benchley brought up a plump hand and brushed at his moustache. "Groucho, you knew me when I was alive, didn't you?"

"We were chums on the sidewalks of New York," Groucho reminded as he struggled to get the pudgy actor to his feet. "Whose robe is that, by the way?"

"Am I wearing a robe?"

"Okay, you're upright," announced Groucho, letting go of him and stepping back.

Benchley teetered, stumbled and started to fall forward. "I have the vague recollection that I was an author of some distinction," said Benchley while Groucho was catching him and pushing him back to a vertical position. "Is that true or merely the vague delusion of a doddering old coot?"

"You were my boyhood idol, Bob, and we all ranked you right up there with Pearl Buck, Albert Payson Terhune and Richard Harding Davis." Groucho eased around until he was standing on the author-actor's right-hand side, then he put an arm around him. "And, although Woollcott never agreed, I thought you were funnier than all three of them put together. And I'll never forget the night we did put all three of them together and Terhune made such a hullabaloo because he was in the middle again." He turned toward Butterworth. "Is he still living in the same bungalow?"

"He was this morning, Groucho."

"I awoke one fine day to discover I'd metamorphosed into an actor," said Benchley, his legs buckling some.

"I've had a similar experience," said Groucho. "Only I used to be a boy tenor."

"I recall that," said Benchley, rubbing again at his moustache. "You were known as the Bobby Breen of our set. Which made it rather hard going for Bobby Breen whenever he dropped in for a visit."

"I'll see you home, Bob."

"Weren't we on some sort of mission, Charlie?" the writer asked his friend. "I remember it was something risky, so I had to fortify myself with strong drink."

"It had to do with Nazimova, as I recall, Bob."

"That's right. Lately I've been getting Natasha Rambova mixed up with Alla Nazimova in my mind," explained Benchley. "One of them lives hereabouts and we decided if we dropped in and took a look at her, that'd settle it once and for all."

"It's Nazimova," said Groucho. "Now let's get you home."

"You're certain it's not Rambova?"

"Certain. In fact, it's one of the few things I'm sure about in this vale of uncertainty."

Benchley considered that information for a few seconds. "Very well, I'll return to my lair and begin a series of short naps," he said, nodding his head. "But, if it's all the same with you, Julius, I'd rather ride in the wheelbarrow."

At about the same time that Groucho was helping Benchley climb back aboard the wheelbarrow, I was also in the vicinity of Sunset Boulevard. After parking my yellow coupe on a side street, I walked along the Strip until I came to the emerald green awning marking the entryway to the Club Tortuga.

There was a tall, thick man in a plaid sport coat and tan slacks leaning against the imitation adobe bricks just to the right of the maroon-colored padded door. "Closed until nightfall, sport," he informed me as I approached the doorway to the nightclub.

"I understand Shel Leverson is here this afternoon," I said. "I'd like to see him."

"Why?"

"It has to do with Peg McMorrow."

"Who're you?"

"Frank Denby." I answered. "I'm pretty sure Vince Salermo has mentioned me to Leverson."

He nodded and said, "Wait." He turned toward the door, started to reach for the handle. Then he thought of something, smiled ruefully and walked over to me. "Just in case," he said and proceeded to frisk me.

Finding no weapons, he returned to the padded door, opened it a few inches and called, "Av, come here a minute, huh?"

A thin, pale man, wearing a double-breasted gray suit appeared in the opening. He and the thickset man had a brief conversation in murmurs I couldn't catch.

The thin man went away and the door slowly closed. "Be a few minutes," the big man told me.

Five minutes later the door opened again and Av, the thin one, made a come-on-in motion at me. "It's okay, Denby," he said in a reedy nasal voice. "He'll see you."

Soon as I stepped into the chill, shadowy foyer, I heard music and the sound of tap-dancing. A small band of five or six pieces was playing a swing version of "The Lady in Red."

A drawling voice suddenly requested, loudly, "Kill the music, Sid."

Everybody but the bass player quit immediately. He went on for another few bars before stopping.

My guide said, "We have to cross the dining room and the show area to get to Mr. Leverson's office."

"Fine." I followed him into the large domed room.

There were no tablecloths on the dozens of small round tables and the spindly-legged chairs had been upended and piled atop them. At the center of the room a small oval area was harshly illuminated by a single white spotlight. Six girls in a variety of rehearsal clothes were lounging in a half circle, watching a small, frizzy-haired man in white ducks and a candy-striped shirt.

He signaled the piano player, a fat man in an overcoat who sat at a white upright on the small elevated bandstand. "Sid, just you on this. Give me the chorus again, if you would."

Sid rested his cigar in an ashtray on top of the piano, ran his tongue over his upper front teeth and went into "The Lady in Red."

The choreographer began a series of energetic dance steps, ending by slapping himself on the buttocks with both open palms. "Is that clear?" he asked the six pretty dancers.

"He's better than they are," commented Av, "which isn't saying a hell of a lot."

We wended our way through a scattering of tables. At a

blank white door, he knocked three times. Then he opened the door and told me, "Go on in."

I crossed the threshold, said "Oops," and nearly stumbled in avoiding the body stretched out a few feet inside the doorway.

Standing beside the large clawfooted mahogany desk was a slim, vaguely handsome man I recognized as Shel Leverson. He was wincing, massaging his right fist. "I lost my temper," he explained, indicating the unconscious thug stretched out on the ivory-colored carpeting. "Now, what can I do for you, Denby?"

Twenty-nine

Like many imported screenwriters, Fredric Weston dressed like an Ivy League professor. He had on a tweed sport coat with leather patches on the elbows, a pair of nubby slacks and tasseled brown loafers.

He and Groucho were seated in canvas chairs in front of his Garden of Allah bungalow. From the unseen swimming pool came shrieks, splashes and laughter.

Taking his pipe from his mouth, the small, tanned Weston sipped his scotch highball. "Drunks," he said disdainfully. "I don't have much use for a man who can't hold his booze. Benchley is an especially annoying example of—"

"He's a very funny man." Groucho, who'd refused a drink, reached a cigar out of his pocket.

The screenwriter shrugged. "I never cared for his pieces in the old *Life* or in the *New Yorker*," he said. "In the movies he comes across, at best, as a gifted amateur actor. Back when he was doing *China Seas* at MGM, he made an absolute fool of—"

"The reason I set up this little rendezvous, Fred, is because—"

"We miss you over at MGM, Groucho. When are you and the boys coming back to make another picture?"

"We've hit a snag with Mayer," said Groucho. "He insists that on all our future movies we have to pay to have the theaters fumigated after each showing." He unwrapped the cigar. "I need some information on one of your fellow writers over there, Fred."

"I'm not much for gossip. Maybe you ought to try Johnny Whistler or that sow Louella."

"I'm trying to find out what happened to Peg McMorrow."

"Is she the cute little starlet who killed herself?"

"I think she was murdered."

Weston chuckled. "You're really a softie, worrying about a minor actress," he observed, trying his drink again. "Most people think of you as a wisecracking cynic."

"No, actually most people think of me as the man who invented the electric light bulb," corrected Groucho as he lit his cigar. "You know Benton McLaughlin, don't you? As I recall, he has the cubbyhole just down the hall from you in the MGM writers' building."

"Known him since Princeton, sure," he answered. "You heard about his wife?"

"Give me," invited Groucho, "your version of what happened to her?"

"Well," said Weston, finishing his highball and setting the glass on the flagstones beside his chair, "the official story is that she went down to Baja a few weeks ago to get away by herself. She simply failed to come back and nobody's been able to find any trace of Babs or her red roadster. Poor Benton's been down there twice, scouring their little hideaway house, talking to the local law, trying to find out something, anything, from the border police." He shrugged and spread his hands wide. "He hasn't learned a damn thing."

"Okay, that's the official story," said Groucho, exhaling smoke. "What do you think really happened?"

Narrowing one eye, the screenwriter watched Groucho for a moment. "How the hell does this tie in with the McMorrow girl?"

"Maybe it doesn't. But tell me anyway."

"Babs, God bless her, has never been known for her faithfulness," said Weston. "I figure, and I don't know who the gent is, she spent the weekend with one of her lovers. Maybe she was in Ensenada and maybe she was really at Pismo Beach or Oxnard."

"That's a long shackup, Fred."

"Could be she decided to run off with this particular lover and simply hasn't gotten around to notifying Benton."

"Has she ever done anything like that before?"

"Not," admitted Weston, "for this length of time. But, yeah, she's been known to disappear for a couple days."

"And what did McLaughlin do about it in the past?"

"You've seen the guy, right? Big husky son of a bitch, Benton is. More than once he slapped Babs around when he found out what she'd been up to—or when she came dragging home and gave him some bullshit story about where she'd been and why she happened to be two days overdue."

"Maybe he did that this time—and went too far."

"Killed her, you mean?" He shook his head. "No, and I admit this sounds goofy, but Benton would never do her any serious harm."

"What about her boyfriends? What did he do to them?"

"He wasn't above threatening a lover, if he knew who it was," said Weston. "And on a few occasions he even decked one of them. You'd think all that violence would've convinced Babs not to stray, but some women just seem born to fool around. You know what I mean?"

Groucho puffed on his cigar. "Ever heard anything linking Babs McLaughlin with Tom Kerry?"

Weston chuckled again. "Sure, but that romance is over," he answered. "Has been for weeks."

"How do you know that?"

"Didn't you hear about McLaughlin's run-in with Kerry a couple months ago?"

Groucho gave a negative shake of his head. "Inform me."

"Well, McLaughlin punched him in the Coconut Grove."

"Oh, my. That's a very painful place to be punched," said Groucho. "And that ended the relationship with darling Babs?"

"Far as I know," answered the writer. "Kerry is pretty heroic on screen, but in real life he's pretty much a chicken."

Groucho leaned forward, asking, "Did the lady take up with somebody else after that?"

Weston glanced around. "Well, I heard a vague rumor," he said. "Sounded strange to me, but you never can tell in this town."

"What?"

"Somebody mentioned seeing her, in an out-of-the-way

joint in the Valley, with the headman from Monarch, old Kurtz-man himself."

Groucho straightened up in the canvas chair. "Interesting," he said, standing and flicking cigar ashes into a nearby shrub. "Ever been up to Lake Sombra?"

"Never," answered Weston, "but I hear it's a great place if you want to shack up in relative privacy."

"I'll make a note of that," said Groucho. "Thanks for this enlightening interlude, Fred."

"Keep me in mind if you're looking for a scriptwriter for your next movie."

"We're not going to use a scriptwriter if we make another one," explained Groucho. "We intend to ad-lib the whole damn thing." He bowed and went slouching off.

Thirty

Leverson settled in behind his massive desk. "Sit down," he invited. "Tell me something."

I inclined my head in the direction of the unconscious hoodlum. "Maybe," I suggested, "we ought to do something about this guy first."

The gambler frowned. "I suppose you're right," he agreed after a few seconds. "Rob—that's Rob on the floor there—is probably distracting." He flicked on his intercom. "Cherry, come in here a minute. I've got something needs to be moved."

Very shortly someone knocked three times on the office door. Then a broad-shouldered man wearing a lime-green polo shirt, tan slacks and a yellow beret came in. "Is Rob the object that needs to be hauled out of here?" he inquired.

Nodding in my direction, Leverson asked, "Don't you think that goddamn hat makes him look like a fairy?"

Sitting in a chair that faced the desk, I scanned the big man. "Nope, not necessarily. Berets are becoming fashionable. In fact, some very masculine guys are now—"

"It makes you look like a fairy," said Leverson. "After you dump Rob in the alley out back, toss the hat in a garbage can."

"I'd prefer to hold on to it, boss, and wear it elsewhere than here." Cherry bent, grabbed up the stunned Rob by the front of his shirt and hefted him clear off the floor. Tossing him over his shoulder, he headed for the door. "The boss has very little fashion sense," he said to me before departing.

As soon as the door closed, Leverson leaned forward. "You came to talk to me about Peg," he said. "So commence."

"Groucho and I think she was murdered," I began.

He made an impatient gesture with his right hand. "You already told Vince that when you guys visited the *Encantada*. Don't you have anything more than—"

"Did you have some of your boys keeping an eye on her?"

Leverson leaned back, causing his swivel chair to squeak. "Not day and night, but occasionally, yeah," he said. "I was still carrying the torch for her, you know, and I sort of wanted to keep up on who she was seeing."

I mentioned the dates we figured Peg McMorrow had been at the Shadow Lodge. "Did you happen to be keeping tabs on her that weekend?"

"Matter of fact, yeah," he said, eying me, frowning. "What's that got to do with anything?"

"Could be nothing, Shel," I answered. "But there's a possibility Peg found out something while she was up there, something that was dangerous for her to know."

"What?" He stood up, planting his fists on the desk and tilting toward me.

"When we find that out, we'll probably know who killed her," I said. "Do you know who she went up there with?"

The gambler scowled. "Yeah, that guy in the tights." He rubbed his thumb and forefinger together, trying to come up with the name. "Actor with the little thin moustache. Kerry. Tom Kerry."

"She was dating Kerry?" I asked.

"Peg was a swell kid," he said for an answer. "But, let's face it, Denby, she was very interested in forwarding her damn career. Hell, I told her we could lean on certain people and get her some star parts, but she wouldn't go along."

"You think she was seeing Kerry so he'd help her get bigger parts and maybe a contract at Monarch?"

The gambler nodded. "I could've done a lot more for her," he said forlornly. "And she'd probably be alive if she'd stuck with me."

"She'd dated Kerry before?"

"Few times. Nothing serious, far as the boys could determine."

"Did your guys notice anything unusual up there?"

"Such as what?"

"Some incident that might've gotten Peg into trouble."

"I'll tell you what happened. I had Cherry, you met him just now, and another guy on that particular tail job," Leverson explained. "They followed her up there, found out she was going to be spending her time shacked up with Tom Kerry. I didn't want a minute-by-minute report of her activities, so they decided to drift over to Reno and hang around there for a couple days. Lot of very nice whorehouses in Reno."

"Too bad they weren't watching more closely."

"If it turns out what went on at the Shadow Lodge had something to do with Peg's getting killed, yeah, it was a mistake not to keep closer tabs on her," he agreed. "But nobody was anticipating that she was going to get killed soon after that."

"Have you talked to Tom Kerry about Peg since her death?"

"I've never talked to that bastard," he said. "I did send one of my associates over to that mansion of his in Beverly Hills. To invite him to drop in, but there wasn't anybody around. Place is shut tight." He nodded twice. "But, sooner or later, we'll track him down. Maybe at that premiere for his new movie that's coming up."

"Do you have any ideas about why she was killed?"

"Somebody wanted to shut her up," he replied. "But I don't know why yet. I'll find out, though. You got anything else to tell me?"

"Not at the moment, no." I got up from my chair. "Thanks for the time, Shel."

"We're on the same team," he reminded, holding out his hand.

I hesitated for a couple of seconds before I shook hands with him. "I guess we are," I said.

The Monarch studios stretch across several acres in Hollywood, just a couple of blocks to the south of Columbia Pictures. A high stuccoed wall, painted a pale peach color, surrounds the Monarch lot and several billboard-size posters decorate the inward-slanting wall. Nearest the gates was a poster, strong with red and yellow, touting the new Tom Kerry epic, *The Pirate Prince.*

I'd parked my coupe in a lot across Gower and approached

the studio on foot. Since I'd used my old *L.A. Times* connections to make an appointment, the guard let me in with no trouble and even smiled at me.

The buildings were stucco and red tile, suggesting a sort of inflated version of the Garden of Allah, with five huge sound stages hulking beyond the offices and administration facilities. Far to the right you could see bits and pieces of the standing sets rising up above the rows of palm trees.

Two pretty girls in bright sarongs came riding by on bicycles along the main street. A guy in a gorilla suit, holding the gorilla head mask under one shaggy arm, was sitting on a metal bench smoking a pipe. Three World War aviators, complete with goggled helmets, were playing catch on a stretch of green lawn. A husky black man in overalls was pushing a rack of ballet costumes along the opposite sidewalk. A half-dozen middle-aged ladies were being given a tour of the studio by a baldheaded man who was using his dead cigar as a pointer.

When I passed the two-story Writers' Building, I noted that an improvised flagpole, flying the Spanish flag, was sticking out of an upper window. From another window dangled a pink, frilly brassiere.

An increasing roar began to fill the air and I looked up to see two biplanes come roaring down through the clear afternoon sky and buzz low over the French Village standing set.

Just as I reached the Publicity Pavilion, the front door flapped open and a pretty blond girl came hurrying out carrying a silver-covered serving dish. She nodded at me, saying, "I know damned well that squinty-eyed little pipsqueak ordered both lettuce *and* tomato."

"Are you alluding to Ira Gruber?" I guessed.

"You must be his one-thirty appointment, huh?" Stopping close to me, she yanked the silver lid off the silver dish. "I'm his damn secretary, which means I have to fetch his lunch from the commissary whenever the mood hits him to dine in. Then, which is worse, I have to schlep it back when his addled little peanut of a brain deludes itself into thinking he didn't order what everybody on the face of God's green earth knows he damn well did order. What would you say are the essential ingredients of a BLT?"

"This is just a wild guess, mind you," I answered. "But probably bacon, lettuce and tomato."

"Well, of course, for Chrissake." She poked a finger at the BLT sandwich resting on the silver plate she was carrying. One bite had been taken out of one of the halves. "But little Mussolini in there now claims he gave me specific instructions to tell those schmucks in the kitchen to hold the damn tomatoes."

"That'd be a BL and not a BLT," I commented. "Shall I go on into Ira's office?"

"Sure, just knock and breeze on in." The lid made a loud clang when she slammed it back atop the sandwich. "He'll be nice to you, since you're from a newspaper. He'll, in fact, kiss your fanny, if you'll excuse the disgusting metaphor." She sighed, went hurrying off in the direction of the studio commissary.

I climbed the red tile steps, pushed into the mosaic-tiled corridor. The first door on my right had IRA GRUBER, CHIEF OF PUBLICITY lettered in three-inch high gilt on the pebbled glass panel. I went in, crossed the empty reception room, knocked on the door to his private office and breezed in.

"That was quick, you dimwitted bimbo. I bet you just plucked the frigging tomatoes off the sandwich with those ungainly meathooks of yours and tossed them in the nearest bush. But that won't work, sweetheart, because I took a hefty chomp out of that sandwich and I'll recognize it if you try to palm it off on me for a second go-round."

I heard Gruber's nasal voice, but didn't immediately spot him anywhere in the huge Swedish Modern office.

"Afternoon, Ira," I said, glancing around. "It's Frank Denby."

His crewcut head popped up from behind his desk. "Frank, old buddy, hey, this is swell." Gruber rose to his full height, which didn't take him that long. He was about five foot four, decked out in a flamboyantly bright Hawaiian shirt and slacks that were pale gold. "So you're back with the old *L.A. Times,* huh? Couldn't cut the mustard as a scripter on the kilowatt circuit, I presume."

"Why were you hiding down behind your desk, Ira?"

"I dropped my pills," he explained as he walked over to one of the high, wide windows and began running a finger up and down over the white metal slats of the venetian blind. "The quack I overpay prescribed something for my nerves."

"I'm still working as a radio writer, Ira," I said and repeated the lie I'd used to get in here. "But I do an occasional Sunday magazine piece for the *Times.*"

"Yeah? I haven't spotted your byline for ages."

"Mostly I work anonymously, so as not to interfere with my new career."

"I hear that hunk of crap you're doing with Groucho Marx is a real turkey."

"On the contrary, Ira," I said. "It's going to be socko, boffo and terrific. To put it mildly."

"If I had to pick, I'd go with Chico Marx to star in a radio show." He came back to his desk, perched on the edge of it. "That wop voice he does is very funny."

"About this latest piece the *Times* wants me to do," I put in. "They're very interested in *The Pirate Prince,* want to give it a big write-up the weekend the picture opens in town."

"So does every other paper and mag in the country."

"What I want you to set up for me, Ira, is an interview with Tom Kerry." I'd decided I wanted to talk directly to the actor and see if I could, as subtly as possible, find out what had happened up at the Shadow Lodge that weekend.

Nodding, the publicity man twisted around and tugged a large pile of manila folders over closer to him. He selected one midway down the stack and slipped it free. Opening it, he scanned the sheets of yellow paper within. "You did me some favors when you were on the paper full-time, Frank," he said. "So I'd like to help you." He shook his head and shut the folder. "Tommy is completely booked up on interviews, from now to the night of the premiere at Klein's Babylonian Movie Palace."

"C'mon, Ira, we're talking about the *Los Angeles Times* here. You don't want to make the Chandlers mad at Monarch, do you?"

He took a quick look toward the window. "Okay, I'll be totally honest with you, Frank," he said. "But this you have to keep strictly under your chapeau."

I nodded agreement, waiting.

"Well, old buddy, it's like this," the publicity man went on.

"Tommy really wore himself down to a nubbin filming *The Pirate Prince.* I know you newspaper guys think this is all bull-shit, but Tom Kerry really does do the majority of his own stunts in these swords-and-tits epics. Old man Kurtzman sent him to his own private doctor right after we wrapped *The Pirate Prince.* The sawbones took one look and prescribed rest and quiet for a couple weeks." He spread his hands wide. "And that, so help me, is gospel."

"Where is Kerry?"

"At a little out-of-the-way place where nobody can find him and pester him for interviews."

"And that part of the gospel you're not passing on?"

"Wish I could, kiddo." He twisted again and tugged out another folder. "Hey, how's this sound? I can let you interview Francesca Sheridan."

"Who is?"

"Don't you keep up with what's going on in this town? She's that gorgeous broad Kurtzman imported from France. Terrific actress and what a pair of knockers she's got on her," said Gruber. "She's making her American film debut in *The Pirate Prince.* She gets her first American screen kiss from Tommy in this one. You'll get more than enough for a swell story if you chew the fat with Francesca."

"Does she speak English?"

"Well, sure, schmuck. Do you think we had Betty Boop in dubbing her dialogue?" Gruber scribbled something on a memo pad with a gold mechanical pencil, tore the page off and handed it toward me. "She'll be at the Coconut Grove tonight and you can interview her to your heart's content—from ten-fifteen until ten thirty-five. After that Johnny Whistler's got her and then Erskine Johnson is coming in to—"

"Okay," I said, "add me to the list." It was a long shot, but maybe Tom Kerry's costar knew something about his activities outside the studio.

There was a knock on the door and the blonde entered with a covered serving dish.

"This is where I came in," I said and left.

Thirty-one

At about two-thirty that afternoon, it occurred to Groucho that he hadn't, to the best of his recollection, had lunch yet. Noticing that he was in the vicinity of the Vine Street Brown Derby, he told me later, he decided to stop in there. Unlike the original Derby down on Wilshire, this one wasn't shaped like a huge hat. It was, like many another Hollywood structure, mostly cream-colored stucco and red tile roofs. There was a large derby-shaped sign mounted on the roof and the words THE BROWN DERBY were inscribed on three sides of the brown awning.

There were, as usual, a few dozen tourists and fans flanking the pathway to the main entrance. As Groucho headed for the wood-framed glass doors, a married couple spotted him.

"It's *him*," insisted the wife, a plump middle-aged woman in a flowered print dress, pointing at Groucho.

"No, it's not. The real one's got a moustache," disagreed the husband, a small, thin man in a tan suit and Panama hat.

Groucho stopped in his tracks, went slouching over to the

woman and took hold of her hand. "You're absolutely right, dear lady," he said in a falsetto voice. "It is me."

She gave him a perplexed look. "Yes, I thought so."

Groucho turned to the husband. "Yes, I am John Gilbert," he told him, still using the piping voice. "The little woman here is absolutely right. You may've heard that my voice ruined me in the talkies, but, as you can see, it has a rich timbre and is extremely masculine. In fact, if I had a few acres of rich timber I could quit this whole lousy movie racket and get back to my first love. Although she may not want to quit the bordello."

"You can't be John Gilbert," said the husband. "He's dead."

"I was dead," admitted Groucho. "But my agent brought me back to life because he was sure he could get me a fat part over at Twentieth-Century Fox. Well, alas, that didn't pan out and now I'm doomed to wander Hollywood for all eternity. It was either Hollywood or purgatory and I figured, if you're going to spend all eternity someplace, heck, you may as well have nice weather." He kissed the plump woman's hand and in his own voice announced, "I must be going."

He loped away.

"That *was* Groucho Marx," said the wife, vindicated.

Groucho pushed into the restaurant and came up against the maître d'. "Top of the afternoon, Bill," he said.

The man's disdainful expression left his face, replaced by a distant smile. "Alone, are we, Mr. Marx?"

"Yes, confound it. Would you believe I couldn't find one underage high school beauty to have lunch with me today?"

The headwaiter chuckled, very briefly, and said, "Table fifty-four all right, Mr. Marx?"

"It's more than all right, William. It's my dream come true."

While heading for one of the low-walled, leather-padded booths on the right side of the Derby, Groucho stopped at a booth where John Garfield was sitting with a sunburned man in a Hawaiian shirt. "Well, hello, Julie," he said, shaking hands with the dark-haired actor.

"Hello, Julius," said Garfield.

"What brings you to this benighted town?"

"Thinking about signing a contract with Warners."

Groucho shook his head. "Have a spinal operation instead," he advised. "You'll enjoy it more." He nodded at the men and continued on his way to his booth.

The afternoon sun was coming in the curtained windows and the framed caricatures of movie stars were glittering on the walls.

At the next booth a redhead who, Groucho was absolutely certain, was wearing not a speck of lingerie, held a telephone receiver in her hand. She made hushing motions at the handsome man opposite her while she talked on the phone. "Yeah, well, Selznick can kiss my fanny," she said loudly. "And so can you, Arnie."

"Hush, quiet," cautioned the man with her. "Don't talk that way to Arnie."

She put her hand over the mouthpiece, saying, "You can take a flying leap for yourself." Back into the phone she said, "I'm insulted that you'd even mention such a pissant salary to me. My nose job cost more than that."

Groucho eased into his booth, then knelt on the seat and gawked over into the booth that held the angry redhead. "If Selznick himself comes on the line," he said, "tell him this for me." He put his thumbs in his ears and waggled all his fingers.

The irate actress put her hand over the mouthpiece again to tell him, "Go poop in your hat."

Feigning a shocked expression, Groucho assumed a more conventional position.

A pretty waitress came over to the table, pencil poised over order book. "How are you today, Mr. Marx?"

"I'm in tiptop shape," he responded with a smile, "considering I just came down with Rocky Mountain spotted fever."

She laughed. "What'll you have?"

"That's a heartless attitude. Especially after I just confided in you that I may only have minutes to live," he complained. "In fact, I'd better order a la carte and skip the dessert. It's no use dropping dead in the middle of a piece of lemon meringue pie."

"The Cobb Salad isn't too bad today."

"For dropping dead in?"

"For eating."

"I don't suppose anybody here has ever heard of a pastrami sandwich."

"They've heard of one, but they sure cannot make one," she said. "How about cold cuts?"

"A bowl of soup," he told her, sighing. "And don't tell me what the soup of the day is, just surprise me. Well, in fact, it won't be much of a surprise anyway, because I saw a big splotch of it on the tie of the cute lad in the next booth. Looked marvelous—robust and hearty. And weren't they a wonderful team, my lands."

She smiled and turned away. "It's split pea."

"That's too obvious even to comment upon," he said, leaning back and tapping his pockets in search of a fresh cigar.

"Well, how nice," said the man who'd materialized at the booth.

"Well, Jack Gardella," he said, recognizing the Monarch Studios troubleshooter. "You're looking more and more like Eddie Robinson every day. I bet you could get a job as his double, if only you weren't so tall and had more hair and didn't have those cauliflower ears and the broken nose."

"This is a nice coincidence," said Gardella, sliding into Groucho's booth uninvited. "I've been wanting to have a little talk with you."

"And I've been wanting to have a little talk with you. Isn't this just delightful. Not to mention delicious and delovely."

Rubbing his hands together, hunching his broad shoulders, Gardella said in his low, raspy voice, "Eli Kurtzman wanted me to talk with you, Groucho. What sort of setup do you and the boys have with MGM? I mean, has Mayer signed you for more pictures?"

"Are you making me a business proposition, Jack?"

"Eli thinks you guys are terrific. If Mayer isn't going to use you any more, Monarch would love to be the new home of the Marx Brothers," he told Groucho. "We figure you haven't even begun to explore the possible locations for further comedies. The opera, sure, and the race track. But how about the fight ring, the baseball diamond, the ice rink?" He framed an imaginary marquee in the air with both hands. "The Marx Brothers in *At the Ballgame.* The Marx Brothers in *At the Prizefights.* The Marx Brothers in—"

"What I wanted to talk to you about, Jack, was—"

"Wait a minute, Groucho. Aren't you interested in making more movies?"

"Actually, I plan to have myself tattooed and then exhibit my body in run-down vaudeville houses and shabby sideshows," said Groucho, unwrapping a cigar. "I'm leaning toward having myself covered from head to toe with scenes from *The Old Curiosity Shop.* When people see the death of Little Nell unfold across my lower back, Jack, there won't be a dry eye in the house. I predict I'll be the biggest thing since Swain's Rats and Cats."

"Kurtzman will double anything MGM can offer, Groucho."

"This wouldn't be an effort to sidetrack me, would it?"

"Sidetrack you from what?"

"Oh, I've developed an interest in the circumstances of Peg McMorrow's death," answered Groucho evenly. "I understand you knew her."

Gardella frowned, shaking his head. "What gossip column did you pick up that bunk in?" he asked. "Naw, Groucho, I never met the lady."

"And Kurtzman never offered her a contract?"

"Are you kidding? She was, as I understand it, a second-rate bit player."

"And you have no idea who killed her?"

"She killed herself, according to the item I saw in the *Times.*"

Groucho said, "Newspaper stories, like gossip columns, aren't always reliable, Jack."

Gardella leaned forward, put his hand on Groucho's sleeve. "Think about our offer," he advised. "And, for your own good, don't go poking into things that don't concern you." He stood up just as Groucho shook free of his grip, left the booth and went striding out of the restaurant.

The pretty waitress delivered Groucho's bowl of soup. "You look unhappy, Mr. Marx."

"Yes," he admitted. "I just realized I wasn't hungry after all."

Thirty-two

By nine-thirty that evening, my interview with Francesca Sheridan was going to be preceded by both a dancing date with Jane and a dinner meeting with Groucho. The three of us arrived at the vast Ambassador Hotel on Wilshire in one of Groucho's automobiles. Being with him assured us a much better reception and a much better table than I could've commanded.

As we were going down the wide carpeted steps to the Ambassador's Coconut Grove nightclub, Groucho, who was decked out in a tuxedo for the occasion, leaned closer to me and said, "Now that I'm a confidential investigator and amateur detective, I've turned over a new leaf."

"Meaning?" I was wearing the better of my two suits and Jane looked great in a simple black evening dress.

"I'm going to be unobtrusive and subdued," he promised. "No use drawing attention to myself while in the throes of an investigation."

"Subdued and Groucho don't go together very well," commented Jane as a very polite waiter showed us to our small table next to a stand of three tall fake palm trees.

"Didn't I tell you to toss this woman overboard, Rollo? She's far too glib." Groucho waited until she was seated and then plopped down in the chair on her left. "Thank you, Henri."

The waiter smiled and bowed. "I'm Maurice, Mr. Marx."

"Ah, that's most unfortunate, most unfortunate," said Groucho. "I've already written you into my will as Henri." He shrugged. "But then perhaps you aren't all that interested in inheriting two pairs of roller skates and a sundial."

The waiter smiled once more. "Would you like to see dinner menus, Mr. Marx?"

"I'd rather see the second act of *Up in Mabel's Room,* but I suppose we'll have to settle for your tatty menus, Maurice."

I was sitting on Jane's other side and scanning the large, high-ceilinged room. There were dozens of small, white-covered tables, each sporting a tiny lamp atop it, and quite a few tall imitation palm trees. Up near the fronds in many of them you could see toy monkeys dangling.

It was still a little early by Hollywood standards and only about half the tables were occupied. The bandstand, which was across the room from us, was empty just now, but the babble and the laughter prevented quiet from closing in.

Tilting in Jane's direction, Groucho asked, "Would you like to dance?"

"If there were music and if it were with Frank, I'd love to."

Groucho lit a cigar, then sighed out smoke. "Well, since there's not going to be any fooling around, we may as well get down to business," he said. "Let's compare notes, Rollo, before it's time for your spurious interview with Fanny Sheridan."

"I've made some notes on what I've come up with today." I reached into the breast pocket of my suit coat for a small packet of file cards. "We can—"

"Groucho! It's wonderful to see you again." Paulette Goddard, blond at the moment, had leaned over and was giving him an enthusiastic hug.

After glancing down the front of her low-cut satin evening gown, Groucho scanned the crowd at the Coconut Grove. "Is Mr. Chaplin with you this evening, my dear?"

"Charlie's meeting with some banker and I'm on my own."

Nodding thoughtfully, Groucho returned the hug. "I notice that the musicians are stumbling back onto the bandstand, Paulette," he mentioned. "Would you care to glide gracefully over the dance floor? Or, better yet, jig disgracefully with your humble servant?"

She laughed, kissed him in the vicinity of the ear and said, "I'd love to, Groucho."

He managed to rise up out of his chair and remain entangled with Goddard. "I do hope they play a tango," he confessed. "I've been told my tango drives women mad."

"I don't mind being driven mad, but try not to tromp on my feet this time." She turned her attention to Jane and me. "You won't be upset, will you, if I borrow him for a while?"

"Just so you don't," said Jane, smiling sweetly, "drag him behind a palm tree and take advantage of him."

Laughing again, Goddard took hold of Groucho's arm. "Come along, Julius."

He nodded at me. "This is a simple operation," he explained, puffing on his cigar. "It'll all be over in a matter of minutes and then we can get back to business."

"Leave the stogie behind," suggested the actress.

He reluctantly deposited the cigar in an ashtray and then headed with her to the dance area. Gus Arnheim's orchestra had just started playing "Harbor Lights."

Jane touched my hand. "Would *you* like to be dragged to the dance floor?"

I stood. "I'll go voluntarily."

This was the first time I'd ever danced with her and I became preoccupied with that for a while. When next I noticed Groucho, he wasn't with Paulette Goddard. He was dancing with Tallulah Bankhead and they actually were doing a tango.

After that I lost sight of him again. When the band went into a Latin American number, a rumba I think it was, I suggested to Jane that we return to our table.

"Here he comes," she said as she sat down and nodded to her left.

Groucho was heading our way, doing a very enthusiastic rumba with Evelyn Venable. As they danced close by us, I heard him saying, "Evelyn Venable, Evelyn Venable. I could go on reciting that till the cows come home. Of course, if you persist in living with cows, I may not drop in at your place much anymore."

He vanished in the dancing crowd after that, resurfacing a few minutes later up on the bandstand. Arnheim borrowed an instrument from his guitar player and handed it over to Groucho. Groucho did the medley of Marx Brothers favorites he'd performed up at Warren Stander's mansion the other day.

"I suppose for him," remarked Jane, "this *is* being sub-dued."

"He's been an entertainer a lot longer than he's been a de-tective," I reminded. "He'll probably—"

"Denby?" A thin man in a tux was standing next to me.

"Yeah."

"You're several minutes late for your interview with Miss Sheridan," he said. "If you want to talk to her at all, I suggest you come with me now."

I got up. "Be back shortly," I told Jane.

"I played saxophone in my high school band," she said. "Maybe I can play some duets with Groucho while I'm wait-ing for you."

Thirty-three

Barefoot, Groucho was pacing slowly on the sandy midnight beach. His black bow tie was untied, his cigar unlit. It was a warm evening and we were about two hundred yards from Jane's cottage. She and I were sitting on the plaid blanket she'd brought down from her place.

Picking up a small flat stone, Groucho sent it skimming across the black water. "Okay, if we put together all the odds and ends of information that we've been digging up these past few days," he said, turning to face us, "we can come up with a plausible scenario. Three weekends ago, Peg goes up to Shadow Lodge with Tom Kerry, possibly for a simple old-fashioned bit of shacking up and mayhap also to try to persuade him to help her get a contract at Monarch. Now Babs McLaughlin is also up there, sharing a cabin with a new lover. We don't as yet know who the lad was."

"But it might be old Eli Kurtzman, the head of the whole Monarch shebang," I suggested.

"Might be the old goat, yeah," said Groucho. "Or it might be Freddie Bartholomew, the Lone Ranger or Evelyn and Her

Magic Violin. We haven't established the identity of who she was domiciled with in that woodland setting."

"But we are sure that Babs and Kerry ran into each other and had an argument," I put in. "Peg's photos prove that."

"Exactly, Rollo," Groucho said, beginning to pace again. "Kerry had been tossed aside by Babs, but apparently was a sore loser. He encounters her in the woods, pleads with her to take him back. She says 'Nertz to you, buster,' or words to that effect. Kerry, like many another ham actor, has a violent temper. He kills the lady and disposes of her body somehow. That explains why she's been listed as missing ever since that fateful weekend."

Jane made a skeptical noise. "Tom Kerry, from all I've heard, and from what you two have been coming up with— well, he isn't an exceptionally tough or forceful guy. Do you really think he's the kind who could kill a woman?"

"Anybody," said Groucho, "can kill anybody, if they're angry enough and go out of control. Happens all the time." He lit his cigar, using a book of Trocadero matches he'd taken from his tuxedo pocket. "Let's just pursue this line of reasoning for a mite longer, lass. Kerry kills Babs, then becomes justifiably upset and nervous. Even in Hollywood, murder can do serious harm to your career. So, he gets in touch with his studio and Kurtzman dispatches Jack Gardella, the trusted troubleshooter, up to Lake Sombra. Gardella tidies things up, maybe even helps hide the body in a nice out-of-the-way spot. It looks very much like Babs actually did drive to Ensenada first, as part of the coverup for meeting whoever it was she was meeting. Gardella probably works at building up the notion that she never left Baja, that something happened to her down there." He blew cigar smoke in the direction of the moderately phosphorescent Pacific. "Only snag is that Peg, probably suspecting something was up when Kerry snuck away for his woodland rendezvous with Babs, followed him with her handy little camera. She sneaks up and gets some shots of them arguing."

"She couldn't have suspected he was going to kill her," I said.

"But, Rollo, she did know that here was a prominent movie star getting together with another man's wife," Groucho reminded. "We have to admit that Peg had a blackmailing streak and she probably took the pictures originally just in case she might be able to use them later on to her advantage. Now, subsequently, when she read in the papers that Babs McLaughlin had supposedly disappeared down Mexico way, she realized that there was some kind of coverup going on. She gathers together a set of her snapshots and approaches somebody at Monarch. Maybe Kerry himself, maybe Gardella—could've been she got to Kurtzman himself somehow. She says, 'I don't want to make trouble for anyone, but it's not going to do dear Tom or *The Pirate Prince* any good if I come forth and say that I know he was with the missing woman just before she vanished.'"

"It's possible," I said, "that Peg actually saw Kerry kill the woman."

"Could be," he conceded. "But if so, why didn't she take pictures of that event?"

"Maybe she did," said Jane. "You fellows only came up with *five* of the shots from her roll of film, remember?"

"That's also possible, Miss Pinkerton," Groucho allowed.

"But all we can be fairly certain of is that she put the bite on somebody at Monarch."

"And then Gardella approaches her and pretends to offer her a contract with the studio," I put in. "That was that night they were spotted having dinner together."

"Actually, he's just stalling her until he can arrange to have her taken care of," said Groucho, frowning. "They kill Peg, swipe the photos and, with the help of crooked cops like Sergeant Branner of the Bayside force, cover the whole thing up."

Jane coughed into her hand. "Where's Tom Kerry?" she asked.

"Eh?" said Groucho.

"Well, from what Frank's been able to find out—including the information he extracted while wrestling with the lovely Francesca Sheridan earlier tonight and calling it dancing—nobody has actually seen Kerry since that weekend."

"I *had* to dance with her," I said in my defense. "That was how she wanted to do the interview and—"

"The young lady raises an interesting point," cut in Groucho. He walked over and squatted on the edge of the blanket. "Why has Kerry been lying low?"

"Maybe he's afraid to face anybody," I suggested. "Scared somebody'll ask him about Babs. Or could be he's afraid that Shel Leverson or some other of Vince Salermo's boys will want to ask him questions."

"It could also be," added Jane, "that he was hurt himself when Babs McLaughlin was killed. If she was killed."

"She has to have been killed," said Groucho. "Otherwise there's no reason to murder Peg to keep her quiet and get those photos. The existing pictures themselves, let me remind you, aren't all that dangerous unless you put them together with what Peg knew."

"We better go up to the Shadow Lodge," I said. "See what can be found out up there."

"An excellent notion," said Groucho, popping to his feet. "We'll do that first thing tomorrow. Will you be able to join us, Janey?"

She shook her head. "Tommerlin's over his cold and I have to be back at his studio tomorrow—fairly early in the day. Sorry, fellows."

"That's as it must be," he said. "We'll forge on alone, side by side, shoulder to shoulder until the flag of our country is again flying atop Fort Sumter. I'll pick you up at about ten o'-clock, Rollo."

Thirty-four

At a little after seven the next morning, Jane appeared in the doorway to her bedroom. "There's a strange creature scratching at my front door," she announced.

I sat up in bed, blinking. "You're not referring to Groucho?"

"No, this is a four-footed strange creature. Come take a look." She was already dressed, wearing a tan skirt and a white blouse.

I hopped free of the tangle of blankets and sheets, tugged on my pants and worked my way into my shirt. Shoeless, I followed her across her living room.

The morning was overcast and out over the ocean gulls were making complaining squawks.

Some kind of claws were scratching at the wooden panels of Jane's closed front door. And there were also low whimpering, slobbering noises to be heard.

I opened the door, gingerly, a very few inches. "Who are you?" I asked the mournful-looking hound who was looking up at me.

He cocked his head to one side, panting enthusiastically.

"Allow me, suh, to introduce you to Dorgan," said Groucho, who walked into view from out of the misty morning. "A genuine southern-fried bloodhound."

I crouched and held out my hand. "Pleased to meet you, Dorgan."

The dog sat and held out a forepaw. "Why are you here, several hours ahead of schedule, Groucho, and accompanied by this cartoon dog?"

"Let me explain the hound first," he said. When he lowered himself onto the top step of Jane's porch next to me, Dorgan waddled over and rubbed against him, licking Groucho's cheek with a long moist tongue. "Save that romantic stuff for later, mutt."

"Good morning, Groucho," said Jane, leaning against the doorjamb and smiling out at us. "What is that thing?"

"Dorgan happens to be a genuine bloodhound," explained Groucho, attempting to dissuade the dog from expressing quite so much affection for him. "I borrowed him from a lifelong chum of mine, whom I've known for well over a year. He trains animals for the films and happens to have this crackerjack bloodhound in his menagerie."

"You intend to take Dorgan up to Lake Sombra with us, huh?" I realized. "To help us search for traces of Babs McLaughlin."

"Actually, Rollo, it turns out that *you* are going to take this worthy canine up to the woodland glades," he corrected. "And to help you in your quest, I'm entrusting to you this handkerchief I purloined from one of Babs McLaughlin's other autos just as dawn was tripping in on little cat feet this morning. Or whatever it is dawn does at such an ungodly hour. Give Dorgan a whiff, then tell him to go find the lady."

"Wait a minute, Groucho," I said, accepting the proffered silk hanky. "As I recall, you were extolling the team spirit only last night. We were going up to the Shadow Lodge area, side by side and hand in hand, to ferret out clues together."

"Well, there's been a change of plans, Rollo, and you're going to have to ferret alone," he said, shaking his head. "As you may've heard, Harpo, also known as the musical Rover Boy, is scheduled to perform this evening at the Hollywood Bowl. Why otherwise rational people would want to sit out in the open air and risk respiratory illnesses merely to hear my brother plunk on a harp is one of the great mysteries of the world."

"So you've decided to attend the concert, is that it?" asked Jane.

"Alas, no, dear child," he said, sighing. "I've allowed my cold, ruthless heart to be melted by the pleas of my hapless sibling. It seems Adolph injured his hand while playing croquet yesterday afternoon with a group of his intellectual chums from the snobbish East." Groucho put a restraining hand on the panting dog and stood up. "I'm alluding to Adolph 'Harpo' Marx and not Adolf Hitler, by the way."

"Come on," said Jane, eying him. "You don't mean that you're going to take his place, do you? If they paid to hear harp music, are they going to sit still for a guitar and selections from Gilbert and Sullivan?"

Groucho pressed a palm over his heart. "You haven't, sweet innocent that you are, grasped the full extent of my perfidy,"

209

he told her. "Nor, for that matter, the full extent of my stupidity. In a rash moment, I agreed to impersonate Harpo."

"Impersonate him?" I said, quite loudly.

The bloodhound's ears pricked up and he glanced at me.

"Can you play a harp?" asked Jane as the dog began to howl.

"Hush, Dorgan," suggested Groucho. "There's no trick to playing a harp, Jane. And, keep in mind, all the Marx boys have an ear for music. However, playing a harp with one's ear is a feat that calls for extreme skill and concentration. I could go on and say something about playing a harp with one's feet, but I'm hoping someone will call a halt to this whole chain of thought."

"You really think you can bring it off?" I asked him.

"I was asked similar rude questions when I announced my plans for flying the Atlantic solo, Rollo," he said. "And that was only last week." He knelt beside Dorgan and glared at him. "Cease this yowling."

The dog stopped and resumed licking Groucho's face.

Jane said, "Frank, you can't drive up to Lake Sombra and back alone and look after that creature."

"If I went on this jaunt," said Groucho, standing again, "it would be impossible to get back to Los Angeles in time for the concert tonight. Besides which, blood is thicker than water. Though nowhere near as good for washing out your delicate things in."

"I'll go along with you, Frank," said Jane. "Unless you two want to postpone the trip until tomorrow."

"Time is of the essence," reminded Groucho. "On top of which, we don't have the use of Dorgan for very long. In two days he's due over at Hal Roach's wickiup to star in an *Our Gang* epic."

When Groucho said *Our Gang,* the dog began to howl again.

I moved over beside Jane. "You can't go with me, you have to report back to Tommerlin and toil away on *Hillbilly Willie."*

"I'll tell Rod I caught his cold and am staying home for a day."

Groucho's eyebrows rose. "I can't believe, Little Nell, that you would tell such a fib."

"Hanging around with you two has eroded my moral sense," she said.

"Ah, you're commencing to sound like my sort of woman," he told her. "Well, my children, I must be going. I popped over bright and early to explain my plight and to deliver this splendid specimen of doghood. If you'd like a splendid specimen of dogwood, along with selected splinters from the True Cross, send ten dollars along with your name and address to the Convent of the Little Sisters of the Poor. Allow five to six weeks for delivery and then forget about the whole darn thing." He bowed toward Jane, patted Dorgan on the head. "Stay, boy, you're working for Master Frank now."

The dog stopped howling and licked at my bare feet.

Thirty-five

We arrived at the Shadow Lodge late that afternoon, just as twilight was beginning to move into the forest of pines, firs and oaks that surrounded the five or so cleared acres that the main buildings and the scatter of cabins occupied. The lake, which was roughly a mile across, was already looking murky as dusk approached and a thin mist could be seen drifting low over the surface.

I'd done the driving and we'd stopped once for lunch and twice to let the bloodhound roam. By the time we reached Lake Sombra, Dorgan was asleep in the rumbleseat, breathing heavily enough so that you could hear him inside the car. There wasn't much else to hear, since Jane and I hadn't been speaking for the past twenty minutes.

Parking in the guest lot to the left of the big two-story red-wood lodge, I turned off the engine and said, "Okay, I'm sorry."

"You don't sound it." She was sitting right against the door on her side of the car, as far from me as possible, with arms folded. "You sound, in fact, extremely insincere."

"You're jaded from living in the vicinity of Hollywood too long. Everybody sounds insincere to you."

"So now are you trying to say that you *don't* think *Hillbilly Willie* is moronic drivel?"

"Look, I was annoyed because you didn't laugh at a pretty funny sequence in the third *Groucho Marx, Master Detective* script," I explained. "That's probably why I made those critical remarks about your strip."

"Hey, it isn't my strip," she corrected, arms still folded. "I only help draw it. However, whatever I may think of Rod Tommerlin as a person—well, I have to admit he's a gifted satirist."

I took a slow breath in and out. Then I bit my lower lip for about thirty seconds. "Fine," I said at last. "We don't exactly agree on that, but there's no reason to—"

"The big mistake, I think, was my agreeing to jot down script ideas for you while you were driving us up here."

"It helped pass the time," I reminded. "Besides which, I have to have the entire damn script done and over to the agency by Tuesday morning."

"I understand that. And, Frank, I am sorry I ripped those three pages out of my notebook, tore them in little tiny pieces and tossed them out the car window into the wind."

I stepped out of the coupe and onto the white gravel. "No great loss," I said. "You're probably right about that stretch of script being unfunny and dull."

"It's funny enough, except for the harpoon gags." She eased out of her side of the car, stood looking up at the rustic lodge. "What I was trying to explain to you before you flew off the handle, Frank, was that I rarely laugh out loud in situations like this. I usually don't even laugh when Rod is trying out *Hillbilly Willie* dialogue on me."

"Right, and that stuff is *really* funny."

"Don't start again," she warned, smiling, "or we never will work out this truce."

I smiled back over the yellow hood of my car. "The feud is over then," I announced. "Although, if you want the damned truth, I am sorry you jettisoned those pages."

"I remember most of the stuff. I'll recreate it once we're in our cabin."

"Great, except leave out the harpoon gags."

"Mr. Denby."

I flinched and took a hopping step forward, then turned to my left. Standing there was a small, freckled man, somewhere in his forties and wearing a crimson and gold bellhop uniform. "You're very light on your feet," I mentioned, eying him.

In a low even voice he said, "I wanted to talk with you before you checked in. I'm Dickerson."

Before leaving Bayside, I'd put in a phone call to Tim O'-Hearn, my Angel's Flight source of information. Even though he hadn't as yet come up with much in the way of further news for me, I asked him if he could find out if anybody working up at the Shadow Lodge might be likely to sell information about past guests and activities at the resort. From our lunch stop I'd phoned O'Hearn again and he'd come up with the name of one of the bellboys, Neal Dickerson. He'd apparently also had somebody contact Dickerson and tell him to expect us.

In case you're wondering, Groucho was financing our overnight stay at the lake and had also provided me with sufficient cash to cover gas, food and bribes.

"You'll be in Cottage Thirteen," Dickerson told me. "It's one of the ones that allows pets and it has a very nice view of the lake in the daytime." He rested the palm of his left hand on the hood of my Plymouth and nodded at Jane. "All you have to do, miss, is go into the lobby there and sign a card. Everything else is all set."

She raised an eyebrow and looked at me. I nodded and she, after a small shrug, climbed up the redwood steps.

Dickerson said, "Very pretty, nice legs. Actress?"

"Cartoonist. Do you have something to tell—"

"Something to *sell,*" he corrected, chuckling very thinly and briefly. "See that boathouse down by the lake? Meet me there at seven-thirty and we can have a nice chat."

When I came back into our cabin at a few minutes before eight, Jane turned away from the front window and let the slats of the blind she'd been holding apart snap back into place. "Well, you survived," she said, "and that creepy bellhop didn't lure you down to that rackety boathouse to murder you."

"Nope, he lured me down there so he could charge me twenty bucks for telling me who Babs McLaughlin spent the fateful weekend with." I lifted a registration card out of my jacket pocket and held it up.

"Well, who was it?"

"A gentleman name of Edwin Kantor."

She blinked, moving closer to me. "Who in the heck is Edwin Kantor?"

"From Dickerson's description, I'd guess Eli Kurtzman," I

answered, putting the card back in my pocket. "You'll notice both gents have the same initials."

"Did the bellboy—seems ridiculous calling him a boy, though—did he know anything about Tom Kerry's activities while Babs was here?"

"He told me that Kerry was indeed here over the same weekend and that he was with a girl who fits Peg McMorrow's description," I said. "But he never saw Kerry and Babs together, nor did he notice any communication between the Kerry-McMorrow team and the Babs-Kurtzman team."

"And the promise of another twenty-dollar bill didn't help?"

I shook my head. "I also asked him if he saw Babs leave here," I told her. "Dickerson says he noticed her car drive off early on that Monday morning, but he won't swear that she was at the wheel. In fact, he thinks maybe there was a man driving."

"Which man? Tom Kerry?"

"Probably wasn't Kerry," I answered. "And he isn't sure if Babs was in the car at all, even as a passenger."

"That's not much information for twenty dollars."

"Well, Dickerson also promised he'd carry our bags out of here tomorrow for no extra tip." I wandered over to the wooden-framed quilted bed. The bloodhound was sprawled at its foot, dozing with his paws in the air. When I sat on the bed, he rolled over on his side and made a snorting sound. "It's possible that the woman never left here."

Jane grimaced. "You want to go hunt for her, huh?"

"Since we've got Dorgan, yeah," I replied. "But you can wait here. I don't plan to start searching the woods until close to midnight."

"Yes, midnight," she said, "that is the traditional time to do spooky things. Anyway, Frank, I am not going to sit here alone again, wondering if somebody's murdering you out in the darkness. I'll tag along."

Thirty-six

At sundown, Groucho was driving up Cahuenga Boulevard, heading for the Hollywood Bowl. The afternoon had become increasingly hazy and the slowly disappearing sun had a bright orange color to it.

On the car radio Johnny Whistler was winding up his evening movie news report. "We hear that the upcoming preem of Tom Kerry's biggest epic yet, *The Pirate Prince,* is going to be gala and then some," he was saying. "Eli Kurtzman, the Monarch mogul himself, is pulling out all the stops. Only snag, so we've been told, is the possibility that the dashing Kerry, suffering from a bad case of overwork, and on the orders of his sawbones, won't be able to attend the festivities at Hollywood's fabled Klein's Babylonian. We'll keep you informed. And finally—an open letter to Al Jolson. Dear Al . . ."

"The things I'd write to Jolson," said Groucho, turning off the radio, "you couldn't broadcast."

Reaching the foothills, he turned onto North Highland Avenue.

The guard at the performers' parking lot said, "Evening, Harpo. I hear you've got a sold-out house."

"I used to have a birdhouse, but after the last sparrows moved out we haven't been able to rent it again."

The guard eyed Groucho. "You know, Harpo, it's amazing how much alike you Marx Brothers look," he said, leaning closer to the open driver-side window. "I ran into that wacky brother of yours, Groucho, a few months ago and the resemblance between you two is uncanny."

Groucho lowered his voice a little and confided, "I'll let you in on a little secret. The Marx Brothers are actually identical quintuplets. But back at the time we were born nobody wanted a set of Jewish quints, so the whole matter was hushed up. Had we but known, of course, I'd be as rich as the Dionne Quintuplets today and, if you want my opinion, I'd look a lot cuter in long curls and a pretty little dirndl than any of those tykes does. And I say that even though I haven't the vaguest idea what a dirndl is." He gave the guard a lazy salute and drove on into the lot.

He parked, tugged a large black suitcase that was splotched with travel and hotel stickers out of the back seat. Groaning slightly, he carried it toward the dressing room area at the rear of the Bowl. The amphitheater covers a sort of natural hollow in the foothills and the stage is shielded in part by a huge concrete band shell that looks like some kind of giant white melon that's been sliced in half.

As Groucho made his way along a corridor, the suitcase banged into the wall and something inside produced a rude honking noise. The dressing room that had been assigned to

Harpo was of modest size and two of the light bulbs in the border that surrounded the makeup mirror were defunct.

Groucho hefted his suitcase up onto the small sofa that sat against the far wall. He opened it and extracted the curly red wig, horn, voluminous overcoat and disreputable hat that his brother had entrusted to him. Extracting his makeup kit, he carried that and the flamboyant wig over to the mirror and seated himself.

He sat staring into the glass, studying his face, for several silent seconds. "Why, Errol Flynn, how did you get in there?" he asked his image. "Oh, silly me. It's actually my own puss I'm seeing." He sighed and leaned back, still looking at himself. "Is this the face that launched a thousand ships? Next time, tell them to use a champagne bottle." After a few more seconds, he said, "Let's try that again. Is this the face that launched a thousand ships? Not to mention three dirigibles, a tuna barge and a garbage scow?" Groucho stroked his chin. "Remind me to have Frank write me some snappy thousand-ships material."

He hunched forward and started to apply his makeup. After he'd darkened his eyebrows, he was about to paint on a moustache when he remembered that he was going to be Harpo tonight. Exhaling slowly, he slapped the wig on his head and adjusted it. When he got the wig sitting just right, he tried the tongue-stuck-in-lower-lip-cheeks-inflated-eyes-crossed expression that Harpo called a gookie.

"You make a very convincing Harpo," he told himself, standing up and away from the mirror. "And if that isn't a sobering thought, I don't know what is."

*   *   *

They didn't start shooting at Groucho until nearly ten minutes later.

Decked out in the full Harpo outfit, with the horn thrust in the waist of his baggy pants, he'd gone up to take a look at the stage.

The members of the fifteen-piece orchestra that was going to accompany him weren't on stage yet, but a uniformed guard was standing just inside the stage entrance that Groucho came slouching through.

"Evening, Mr. Marx," he said.

Groucho waved, honked his horn and kept moving.

"Yikes," he observed, having forgotten that using a horn that's stuffed in your pants can send a blast of air straight into your crotch.

Walking a bit gingerly for a moment, he went over to inspect the harp that he was going to have to wrestle with during the concert. It sat at the front of the Bowl stage.

The many rows of seats that fanned out across the open-air theater were all empty and twilight was filling the area. While the stage was fully illuminated, few of the audience lights were on yet.

Hands behind his back, slightly crouched, Groucho circled the harp. "Let's see now," he muttered, "how exactly do you play one of these damn things?"

"And just who might you be?"

"I might be Dame May Whitty if only the job paid a little better than it does."

A hefty middle-aged man in white tie and tails was glowering at Groucho, hands on hips. "You're not Harpo Marx," the man accused.

Groucho noticed the baton clutched in the man's right hand. "Ah, you're Maestro Busino," he realized. "Allow me to introduce myself."

"You're not Harpo Marx."

"Yes, my mother was always complaining about that, too," admitted Groucho, adjusting his red wig. "But my response was 'How many Harpos do you want in one family?' "

"We have hundreds upon hundreds of people due to arrive here within less than two hours," the orchestra leader informed him angrily. "And instead of Harpo Marx, we have a shabby imposter."

"Have a care, sir," said Groucho, standing up straight. "I may be an imposter, but I'm far from shabby. In fact, the last time I looked at a map I was seventeen miles from shabby and just over the hill from the poorhouse." He held out his hand. "I'm Groucho Marx and I can explain everything."

Busino leaned forward, eyed him. "Yes, you are Groucho," he said, smiling some and shaking hands. "But we're scheduled to do a concert with your brother, Harpo."

"Perhaps we should have alerted you, Maestro," admitted Groucho. "But, well, we're a wild, scatterbrained clan, we Marxes. As anyone in the highlands of Scotland will readily attest."

"Where's Harpo?"

"He injured his hand in a brawl in a cantina down in Tijuana, although he's claiming he did it playing croquet," said Groucho. "Our plan for the evening is this—and Harpo wanted it to be a surprise and I went along with him, Maestro—you introduce me as Harpo and I play a few of his standard pieces."

"You can play the harp?"

"Like a native," he assured the uneasy musician. "All right, I do a few numbers, the audience is enthralled, maidens swoon. About that time, the real Harpo comes out on stage and yanks off my wig while handing me a guitar. He exhibits his bandaged hand and I explain, in tones that will bring tears to the eyes of the easily swayed, that my dear sibling is in-jured—unfortunately not fatally—and that I filled in for him. He'll don the costume, I'll play the guitar and he'll do a few stunts that don't involve playing a harp. Now, for the grand fi-nale—if Harpo succeeds in prying him loose from a bridge game over at L. B. Mayer's shanty—Chico will appear and do his same old annoying tricks on your piano." He paused, spread his arms wide and curtsied. "We thought it might be en-tertaining."

Busino chuckled, nodding approvingly. "Yes, it definitely will be," he agreed. "But you should have told me."

"That tends to spoil the surprise, we've found."

Nodding, the leader said, "I won't tell the members of my orchestra. And I'll introduce you as Harpo Marx."

"Splendid and now—"

A bullet came whizzing down out of the dusk and they heard the crack of a rifle shot.

Not hit, Groucho threw himself flat out on the stage. The horn at his waist gave a gasping honk and another bullet rushed close by him.

Thirty-seven

Just shy of midnight, I awakened Dorgan and hooked him up to his leash. Then I encouraged him to sniff the Babs McLaughlin handkerchief that Groucho had purloined.

The bloodhound, after doing an enthusiastic job of sniffing, lunged for the door of our rustic Shadow Lodge cabin.

Jane turned off our lights while I held Dorgan back, then opened the door a few inches.

There were no outdoor lights down at this end of the property and only misty darkness showed outside.

Carrying the small flashlight and short-handled spade we'd brought along in the rumbleseat with the borrowed dog, Jane stepped, very carefully and cautiously, out into the foggy night.

Dorgan and I followed.

Two cabins away someone was playing Bing Crosby's record of "I Surrender, Dear" on what sounded like a very old wind-up Victrola.

"Do you really think," asked Jane in a whisper, "that the McLaughlin woman is buried hereabouts?"

"It's a possibility we have to look—"

The hound had been vigorously sniffing at the air. Suddenly he went padding off to the left, head down, nose snuffling at the ground. Since I was attached to him by a short length of leather leash, I went along.

Jane caught up with us just as Dorgan pulled me into the woods beyond the farthest cabin. "I'm feeling extremely uneasy," she confessed, walking beside me on the mossy trail.

"The anticipation of unearthing a corpse late at night makes most everyone feel uneasy," I told her, taking hold of her arm with my free hand.

"Maybe so, but I'm experiencing the sort of goosebumps you get when somebody's watching you."

"We followed a pretty roundabout route our first hour driving up here out of L.A.," I reminded. "And neither one of us spotted anybody following our car, nary a soul."

"Suppose somebody was already up here, waiting for intruders?"

"Oh," I said quietly. "I hadn't thought of that."

"Well, that's what I've been thinking about."

"Dickerson the overage bellboy would've told me if—"

"This is the same overage bellhop who sold you a guest's registration card for twenty bucks, isn't it?"

"You're right, Dickerson may not be exactly one hundred percent trustworthy."

The bloodhound had been progressing more slowly into the woodlands for the past minute or so. He halted completely now, looking around at the dark oaks and pines we were in the midst of. Then he lurched to the right, leaving the trail completely to go barging into the brush.

Nearly ten scratchy minutes later, after dragging me

through nettles, brambles, over fallen trees and by something that couldn't have been but certainly felt like cactus, he came to a stop in a small clearing in the night woods.

"I haven't been on a hike like this since I quit the Girl Scouts," said Jane when she caught up with us.

Dorgan was very fretful. He started circling a patch of ground at the far side of the clearing, ground that was covered over with dead leaves and dry twigs.

Then, as Jane turned the beam of the flash on that spot, the dog began scratching at the ground. He got the cover of leaves and dry brush cleared away and went to work with his paws on the moist ground below.

Moving closer, I said, "Looks like part of the ground under here has been disturbed lately." Working in a sort of partnership with Dorgan, I uncovered a large section of recently turned earth.

"Disturbed by the digging of a grave, you mean?"

I stood up and back. "Well, it's about the right dimensions. Six feet by three feet." I pulled back on Dorgan's leash to keep him from digging deeper. "Whoa, boy. I'll take over."

"You're supposed to say 'Whoa' to horses, not bloodhounds."

"Since you're an expert on animal husbandry, you hold him while I start digging."

She exchanged the spade for the leash. "Sit, Dorgan, sit."

Very reluctantly, the dog backed away and sat on the ground, making sad, whimpering noises.

I scrutinized the possible grave site and decided to start shoveling at the right-hand end.

In roughly fifteen minutes I was looking down on the dirt-covered outline of the head and shoulders of a corpse. "Now comes the even more gruesome part." I set the spade aside, tugged out my pocket handkerchief and knelt beside the body. I took a deep breath of foggy night air, exhaled it slowly and gingerly started brushing the last of the earth off the dead face.

Jane had moved nearer and was shining the flashlight directly into the shallow grave.

"Frank!" she said when the features were showing.

There'd been quite a bit of deterioration, but you could still recognize the corpse. It wasn't Babs McLaughlin.

"That's Tom Kerry," said Jane softly.

Earlier, at the Hollywood Bowl, Groucho had stretched out on the stage and attempted to make himself as flat as possible. Three more rifle shots had come flying at him.

All missed, though one went clean through the hat that had fallen off his head when he'd dived for the floor.

The uniformed guard had yanked out a pistol after the first shot and come running to the edge of the stage. "There he is," he shouted, firing his .38 into the far darkness. "Way the hell up there."

Two more guards had materialized out among the seats and were running uphill in pursuit of the gunman.

Groucho, still sprawled, narrowed his left eye and looked out at the rows of empty seats. "Worst audience response I've had since we played New Castle, Pennsylvania, in the autumn of 1916," he said.

"Up that way, cut the bastard off!" another of the guards was calling out.

The guard from the stage had dropped off into the aisle below and was running up it.

The orchestra leader, who'd also thrown himself to the stage at the sound of the first rifle shot, sat up. "Are you all right, Groucho?"

"No bullet holes," he replied. "Although my morale is at a low ebb just at the moment. Yourself?"

"Unhurt, thank you." Busino rose to his feet, walked to the edge of the stage to squint out into the gathering night. "I think your assailant got away into the brush beyond the furthermost seats."

A bit shakily, Groucho became upright again and then bent to scoop up the injured hat. "I suppose a bullet hole adds a touch of mystery to this headpiece." He tugged it back on top of his bewigged head, frowning.

Two of the guards were walking dejectedly back toward the front of the Bowl. "Lost him," one of them called through cupped hands.

"Why would someone want to shoot Harpo Marx?" the conductor asked.

"I think this particular marksman wanted to bag me, Maestro."

Busino looked puzzled. "But nobody knew you were going to be taking your brother's place here tonight."

"On the contrary," said Groucho. "A select handful of people did. What I have to do now is find out in whom they confided."

"After this outrage, we'll have to postpone the—"

"Like hell we will," cut in Groucho. "The show will go on

as planned. Nobody else is going to try to take potshots at me tonight, I'm sure."

"Well, that's a very brave and courageous attitude, Groucho."

"Forget courage and bravery," he said. "Once I take this Harpo outfit off, I don't intend to put it on ever again. If I don't do this tonight, I never will." He reached into his pants pocket for a cigar. "Now show me where I can find a telephone. One I don't have to drop nickels in, by the way."

Thirty-eight

Jane looked away from the movie actor's grave. "I was expecting someone else," she said slowly.

Turning my back on the actor's body, I said, "Wonder why the dog led us here. He had a whiff of Babs McLaughlin's handkerchief, not anything that belonged to Tom Kerry."

"Well, we know Kerry and Babs McLaughlin spent some time together," she said. "Probably her perfume or her scent is clinging to him."

I walked over closer to the grave. "Are they both dead? Is she buried around here, too?" I asked. "Or even in this same spot?"

"Don't bother digging for her," advised a voice from the misty woods. "She's not here."

Dorgan rocked to his feet and started barking.

Jane moved nearer to me as two men, neatly dressed in business suits, stepped into the foggy clearing from among the blurred trees.

One of them held a .45 automatic, the other a smaller gun that I couldn't identify but I guessed was probably of European make. The taller of the pair had his pale blond hair cropped very close. His companion was thin and frail-looking with slicked brown hair and a faint moustache. I'd never seen either of them before, on or off the screen.

"I told you I had the feeling somebody was watching us," said Jane quietly.

"You wouldn't be working for Vince Salermo?" I asked them hopefully.

"No, sorry." The taller man was the one who'd spoken before.

The bloodhound kept barking at them, straining at the leash Jane was holding onto.

"Keep the pup silent," suggested the frail man, gesturing with his gun in Dorgan's direction.

"Quiet, boy." Jane tugged on the leash. "Sit."

Grudgingly, Dorgan complied.

I nodded at the partially buried body. "That some of your work?"

"No, certainly not." The crewcut man shook his head and smiled. "We're, let's say, something in the way of being custodians of the poor chap's temporary resting place."

His associate moved his thin shoulders up and down. "Too much conversation going on," he complained, impatient.

"You're absolutely right," the other agreed. "We'll have to, I'm very much afraid, ask you to accompany us."

"Listen, that's not going to work," I began. "The people at the lodge know we—"

"Too much conversation." The frail man all at once sprang toward me.

"Frank!" Jane yelled. "Look out!"

Before I could dodge, he used the butt of his gun as a club and hit me hard across the base of my skull.

I managed to form my right hand into a fist, but never got to swing at him. I heard the dog bark, felt the gun sap me twice again, was aware that Jane was crying out. After that I didn't notice anything except the darkness.

Very slowly, I became aware of a sad, whimpering sound.

At about that same time, I realized that I was in the grip of a very intense headache and that just about every bone in my body was aching. I could feel my pulse throbbing in all sorts of new and unexpected spots.

The whimpering continued, but I was pretty sure I wasn't doing it. I seemed to be sitting in a hard wooden chair and I didn't feel like opening my eyes just yet.

"Frank, are you okay?"

That sounded quite a lot like Jane.

After contemplating the chore for a moment or two, I started opening my eyes.

That turned out to be a mistake, because it let in all the harsh yellow light that filled the room. The glare came rushing into my skull, making my headache even worse.

I shut my eyes and gasped in a breath.

"Um," I managed to say.

"Frank," said Jane, "I'm over here."

I made another effort and got my eyes open again. This time the light didn't bother me as much and I didn't have to shut them.

We were in the living room of a cabin with log walls. Dirty

white window shades kept out the night. Jane, her hair tangled and her face streaked with dirt, was in a straight-back wooden chair in front of the small empty stone fireplace. I finally comprehended that she was tied securely to the damned chair with a coil of thick, greasy rope.

When I tried to get up and go over to her, I discovered that I was tied down, too. "They must've gotten a great deal on greasy rope," I muttered. "Where exactly are we, Jane?"

"Other side of the lake," she told me. "Isolated cabin in the woods. They brought us across in a motor launch."

"Who's that whimpering?"

"Dorgan," she answered. "They locked him in the kitchen."

"You goddamn assholes," said another woman's voice. "I hope you're satisfied with the mess you've made of everything."

Frowning, I very slowly turned my damaged head to the left.

There was a dark-haired woman in her early forties tied to a chair over against the wall.

"We've found Babs McLaughlin," said Jane.

Thirty-nine

Right leg tucked under him, left leg dangling, Groucho was perched on the edge of the large wooden desk that belonged by day to the artistic director of the Hollywood Bowl. His Harpo wig and the bullet-riddled hat sat near his backside and the horn was resting atop the swivel chair.

He was talking into the phone. "Zeppo, strive to keep your fiery temper under control," said Groucho, striking a match with the thumbnail of his free hand and lighting his cigar. "No, nay, I'm not accusing you of being an assassin . . . Well, at least not of attempting to assassinate me earlier in the evening. Who you assassinate on your own time is a matter of supreme indifference to me and . . . No, I'm not saying I'm indifferent to you . . . No, you are not my least favorite brother. In truth, Zeppo, you happen to be one of my four favorites among the brothers. Yes . . . now, please, attend to me. You also happen to be, in addition to an esteemed sibling and companion of my youth, one of only three other schmucks who actually *knew* in advance that I was going to be impersonating Harpo here tonight . . . What do you mean why didn't I let one of your clients fill in for him? I *am* one of your clients. Although you haven't gotten me a lick of work since I did that split week as a carhop in Pasadena and Altadena two months ago . . . But let's cease dodging the issue . . . Who did you happen to tell about my . . . No, Zeppo, I'm not accusing you of plotting behind my back. Come to think of it, however, there's more than enough room back there for picnics and business gatherings and maybe even a rump convention . . . Concentrate now, to whom did you talk about my night of shame here at the Bowl? . . . I already talked to Harpo and Chico and they . . . How's that again? You openly mentioned the fact of my impersonation to one Marliss Reggal? And who or what is that? . . . An upcoming young actress. Oh, it sounded like a new brand of beer. Where did she wander and roam after you blurted out this family secret to her? . . . Ah, I see." Groucho grinned and exhaled a swirling cloud of cigar smoke. "Little Marliss had a screen test early this afternoon over at the Monarch studios. Monarch, where Eli Kurtzman, Jack Gardella and sundry other goons roam. Where, I'll bet, they know how to hire a lunkhead who's an expert with a high-powered rifle. Well, not that much of an expert, since he missed everything but my hat. And, by the way, the next time anybody sends an assassin after me, I'd prefer that he use a low-powered rifle. Much safer and . . . What tendency to babble? If I were any more silent and self-effacing, Zeppo, I'd be a wallflower. What? . . . No, I don't think the fact that some vindictive goniff tried to gun me down would make a nice item for Louella Parsons or Johnny Whistler or . . . Well, if Louella needs something about me for that collection of tripe she and Willie Hearst call a column, tell her that I've just had my hair dyed an absolutely lovely shade of lavender and am set to star in the upcoming *Oscar Wilde Rides Again* serial over at Republic. I play the one on the bottom . . . Thanks for your help, brother dear. But next time, to quote the great Oriental philosopher, Key Luke, keep your lip buttoned. Farewell." He hung up the telephone, dropped free of the executive desk and put the wig and hat back on.

Gathering up the horn, he carefully inserted it in the waist of his rumpled trousers. "We really are going to have to do something about old Eli Kurtzman and his merry men," he said aloud, heading back for the Hollywood Bowl stage. "And soon."

The concert was a success. In fact, when Groucho, Harpo and Chico took their final bows, they got a standing ovation from the enthusiastic crowd. Groucho was of the opinion that this had less to do with their combined talents than with the fact that, according to him, the Hemorrhoid Sufferers of America had booked a large block of seats for the show and reached the point by the finale where they couldn't bear to sit down any longer.

He mentioned that fact to the reporters who were waiting for him outside his dressing room, but it failed to divert them.

"Who tried to shoot you, Groucho?"

"We suspect sibling rivalry," he said, his back against the door. "Right now the prime suspects are the Ritz Brothers, the Boswell Sisters and the Dionne Quintuplets."

"C'mon, be serious," suggested a newsman from the *Herald Examiner.*

"I'm glad you mentioned that," said Groucho, taking out a fresh cigar. "This is as good a time as any to announce that I've been asked to star opposite Norma Shearer in *King Lear.* We intend to flip a nickel—which Louis B. Mayer has kindly agreed to loan us at a very small interest rate—to decide who'll be Lear and who'll be the Fool. I think I'd make a dandy King Lear because I already have the beard. Later on, if you're all really nice to me, I might even show you that beard. And now, gentlemen of the press, it's—"

"This crazed assassin," put in a reporter from the *Hollywood News.* "Was he after you or after Harpo? According to eyewitnesses, you were wearing that Harpo disguise when the killer made his try for you."

"Fellows, you know that I delight in cooperating with the papers," said Groucho patiently. "Why, only last week I gave Louella Parsons a complete rundown of my bowel movements for the month of July. I don't see how I can be any more open and forthcoming than that. So you'll have to believe me when I tell you that I have absolutely no idea who the fellow with the rifle was nor why he was Marx hunting here at the Bowl. Official Marx Brothers season, by the way, doesn't open for another week. So, when they catch this lad, he's going to face having his license lifted."

"Was it an irate husband?" asked a heavyset reporter that Groucho didn't recognize.

"I assure you that my husband is completely satisfied with me." Groucho reached behind himself and got hold of the doorknob.

The *L.A. Times* man told him, "If you're covering up something, Groucho, we're eventually going to find out. Why not tell us the truth now and save yourself a lot of trouble?"

"How come you haven't found out why my paperboy keeps tossing the *Times* in the fishpond instead of up on the porch most days?"

"Boys, that's enough questions for Mr. Marx right now." Two uniformed deputies from the sheriff's office were standing there among the scatter of reporters.

"What can *you* tell us about the shooting incident?" asked the *Times* man.

"The sheriff will have a statement later on." One of the deputies, a large, wide, tanned young man, nodded at Groucho. "If you'll step into your dressing room, sir, we'd like to have a few words with you."

"Let's see you be funny with these boys," said the *Herald Examiner* reporter disdainfully.

"If you want to see that, you'll have to buy a ticket." Groucho, his cigar still unlit, wiggled his way into the dressing room.

Toward the end of Groucho's nearly half-hour detailed interview with the deputies, a tall, thin man in an overcoat and gray fedora slipped into the room. "Don't let me bother you," he said, smiling thinly.

"What's your interest in this, Branner?" asked the tanned deputy.

"Ties in with something we're interested in over in Bayside maybe." He took a crumpled pack of Camels out of his coat pocket and shook a bent cigarette into his hand. "Mind if I smoke?" he asked, lighting the cigarette.

"Should I know who this fellow is?" inquired Groucho. "Or is he just somebody they sent over because they ran out of smudge pots?"

"You're an extremely witty man, Marx," said Sergeant Branner. "I'm Branner, Bayside police. Maybe your partner, Denby, mentioned me to you."

"He did, but I didn't recognize you without your bunch of bananas."

Branner blew out smoke and grinned lopsidedly at the two men from the Sheriff's Department. "What did I tell you? A very funny man, he is."

When the deputies left, Branner remained leaning against the wall and smoking.

"Am I wrong," asked Groucho, "or don't you have any jurisdiction in this part of L.A.?"

Branner spread his thin hands wide. "I only dropped by to give you some advice, Marx," he said.

"We already get our advice from Dale Carnegie." Groucho had gotten out of the Harpo getup while he was being questioned by the sheriff's deputies. He was wearing his own clothes again. "So if you'll toddle along, Sergeant, I'll change my venue."

"This is all I have to pass along to you," said the Bayside cop patiently. "There are people out there who simply don't like you. The reason for that dislike is simple—you insist on poking your nose into something that doesn't have a damn thing to do with you."

"Were you the lad with the rifle, Branner?"

The sergeant chuckled. "You'd be on a slab now, Marx, if I'd shot at you," he assured him. "Forget this whole business. Stick to the movies."

"Everybody who had anything to do with Peg McMorrow's death," said Groucho evenly, "is going to come tumbling down, Branner. You really ought to think about finding a nice safe place to hide."

The lean policeman dropped his cigarette butt on the floor, ground it out with his heel. "And you, Marx, better start thinking about burial plots." He left.

Groucho turned and looked at himself in the mirror. "Boy, I sure hope you weren't bluffing," he said to himself.

Forty

A few minutes before the fire started the bloodhound quieted down.

Perhaps he'd decided, as I was on the verge of doing, that things were pretty near hopeless.

"Kill us?" I asked Babs McLaughlin. "All of us?"

"Aren't you hearing what I'm saying, shithead?" she inquired, leaning against the ropes that bound her to the chair. "The situation was starting to look okay for me—until you two jerks stumbled in. I think I could've eventually persuaded the old fart to simply trust me. Then it would've been easy. He'd send me to Mexico for a few weeks." She shook her head, scowling at me. "After that I would've come staggering out of a convenient patch of jungle one day and claimed I'd been kidnapped from Ensenada and had been suffering from amnesia until just that minute. Would've worked."

Jane said, "We've been operating on the assumption, Mrs. McLaughlin, that you'd been murdered up here—probably by Tom Kerry. That's why we—"

"Came snooping around up here with a goddamn bloodhound. Jesus, how corny can you get?"

"Since, if I'm interpreting this correctly," I said, "you think we're all about to be executed—suppose you tell us exactly what went on three weekends ago?"

"What good'll that do?"

"Not much, but I'd like to know who did what before I shuffle off."

She sighed and gave me another scowl. "I don't know how much you've heard about me," she began, "but I'm sort of restless."

"We've heard," said Jane.

"My husband calls me an unfaithful slut, but I think that's a bit harsh. Restless is a better term and—well, if you've ever spent any time with Benton, you'll understand how very easy it is to get restless when you live with a man like that."

"Who did you come to the Shadow Lodge with?" I asked Babs.

"With the old fart."

"Eli Kurtzman?"

"That old fart, yes. I find that guys his age can be extremely grateful—in a financial way—for relatively small favors."

I was pushing my arms against the ropes as we talked, trying to loosen them. "Where does Tom Kerry fit in?"

"Tom's an old beau of mine, but that pretty much ended months ago," she said. "Do you have to fidget like that?"

"I'm bound for glory, ma'am. I might as well fidget while I can," I told her. "On top of which, I'm attempting to loosen these ropes."

"Fat chance you'll have of that," she said. "So Tom showed

up with that pesty Peg McMorrow, but he kept ditching her and sneaking visits with me whenever Kurtzman was off somewhere. When you shack up with old Eli, you have to leave him plenty of time to go phone the studio and the bankers and the New York office." She shook her head. "At first I told Tom to just simply leave me alone. But then—"

"Peg got some pictures of one of your arguments," I put in. "That's why she's dead."

Babs frowned. "They did kill her, then? Eli told me she was trying to blackmail him and—well, he made some nasty threats, but I wasn't sure what they eventually did to her. She was a mean-minded little bitch, but . . ." She shook her head again. "Anyway, I let Tom persuade me to spend a couple of hours with him. In this very cabin, actually. It belongs to some friend of his who's in Europe, but he wasn't staying here with Peg McMorrow. No, they had a cabin over at the lodge and this hole he saved for me. Well, Eli found out about it and came busting in. Him and that gorilla who works for him. Jack Gardella. I think—probably—that originally Eli was only intending to have Gardella beat Tom up a little."

"Rough up his major star?" I asked. "That's not smart business."

"Have I mentioned that Eli can be—much like my damned husband—extremely jealous," Babs said. "Tom was a jerk in many ways and when Eli and his boy came storming into the bedroom here, he made the mistake of taunting the old fart. You know, telling him that I had to turn to him for any real sex and so on. That set Eli off and . . ." She paused, closing her eyes. "Eli had a gun, a thirty-two revolver, I think. He pulled it out and, before Gardella could grab his arm, he shot Tom.

Twice—" She lowered her head, pointing at her chest with her chin. "Two times in the chest. I got blood all over me."

"That's a shame," said Jane. "But since you were probably naked, at least it didn't soil your good clothes."

"Hey, asshole, quit razzing me. Christ, I've been holed up in this crappy rat trap of a cabin for weeks now," she said. "With four of Eli's toadies looking after me and making damn sure that I don't get away or blab to anybody about what went on."

"Have you talked to Kurtzman since the killing?" I asked her.

"Twice, yes," Babs replied. "He's been saying he just wants to keep me out of sight until he arranges everything. They're going to move Tom's body soon now and then plant stories that he had some kind of breakdown and has dropped out of sight. Eli figures people forget movie stars pretty quickly."

"You and Gardella are the only actual witnesses to his killing Kerry," I pointed out. "I imagine he trusts Gardella, but why would he trust you?"

"He doesn't anymore," she complained. "Thanks to you."

"What," asked Jane, "do we have to do with your problem, Mrs. McLaughlin?"

"The last time Eli was here, nearly a week ago, we had a fairly friendly talk," she said, anger in her voice. "I'd pretty near convinced the old fart that I wasn't going to tell anybody about what'd happened *and*, unlike dear Peggy, I'd never try to blackmail him."

"Peggy couldn't really prove anything had happened up here," I said.

"Peggy may've thought that it was the other way around,

too. That Tom had killed me in a jealous rage," she said. "But it didn't matter. She knew Eli and I were up here, she knew I'd been with Tom. When I was reported missing, she must've figured she had a chance to blackmail herself into better parts and more dough. If she had talked to reporters—well, it would've meant trouble for Kurtzman and Monarch. He's a powerful son of a bitch, but he can't bribe the whole damned press in California, especially when you're talking about a box office star like Tom. It was simpler to kill her and cover it up."

"And that's what you think is going to happen now?" I asked in a small voice. "They're going to knock us all off and rig it to look like an accident?"

"It's what I *know* is going to happen," she said. "While you were being hauled over here from the other side of the lake, I heard the other two talking. They'd contacted Eli as soon as they found out you were up here. He apparently told them that it was too dangerous to let me live, now that so many people were in on this. So we're all three on the way out." She shook her head again. "I wouldn't bet that your pal Groucho Marx is going to reach a ripe old age either."

Jane was looking toward the door that led to the kitchen. "Dorgan is whimpering again," she said. "But it's different than before. He's upset about something new."

"Where are these four goons?" I asked.

"I haven't seen any of them since you two were delivered here."

Jane said, "They knocked me out, too, Frank. But I came to earlier than you did."

I was sniffing, tilting my head slightly forward. "I smell something."

245

"Jesus," said Babs, starting to struggle against her bonds. "It's smoke."

"They're going to burn the cabin," said Jane.

In the silence you could hear the flames start to crackle around the outside of the wooden house.

Forty-one

A man answered the phone. "Yeah?"

Very politely, Groucho requested, "I'd like to speak to Marliss Reggal, please."

"Listen, buddy, it's almost midnight and if you think—"

"Tell her this is Groucho Marx." He was sitting at the desk in his den, a homemade pastrami sandwich resting on a plate near the phone. "My brother Zeppo is her agent and—"

"How the hell do I know you're really Groucho Marx? Anybody can claim—"

"Well, I have a strawberry birthmark on my backside," Groucho told him. "And a cute little scar right across here. Right now I'm wearing a tatty blue bathrobe, smoking a King Edward cigar and planning to eat a pastrami on Russian rye. Does that answer the description you have?"

After a few seconds the man who'd answered the starlet's phone grunted. "Maybe you are him," he conceded. "Hold your horses and I'll get Marliss."

Groucho was able to take two slow bites of the sandwich before a young woman with a slight southern accent came on the phone. "Yes, Mr. Marx? I'm terribly sorry if my cousin was rude to you," she apologized. "He's very protective."

"Think nothing of it, my child. Everybody is rude to me," he assured her. "I wanted to ask you about your afternoon over at the Monarch cinema factory."

"Why, that's very nice of you to take an interest in my career, simply because your brother happens to be—"

"I am deeply interested, Marliss," he said. "But right now I'm curious as to whom exactly you chatted with whilst there."

She inhaled sharply. "Oh, does this have something to do with your being shot? I heard about that on the radio only a few—"

"This is just a routine series of questions," he told her, borrowing a line he'd heard recently in a Pat O'Brien cops and robbers movie. "Can you remember anybody you might've told that I was substituting for Harpo at the Hollywood Bowl tonight?"

"Well, there was the girl—I think her first name is Georgine—who helped me put on makeup for the test," answered the young actress. "And later on, after they'd shot the scene I had to do, one of the important executives came in to the sound stage to congratulate me."

"And that was?"

"Somebody told me afterward that it was Jack Gardella. He's a big man at Monarch and—"

"He'd heard about what you'd told Georgine and wanted details?"

"Yes, that's it exactly, Mr. Marx," she said. "You don't think that Mr. Gardella could've had anything to do with—"

"No, certainly not. As I said, this is just a routine thing the police asked me to do, Marliss."

"Everybody said the test came out very well, Mr. Marx," she said. "So if you and your brothers ever do manage to make a comeback in the movies, why, keep me in mind, huh?"

"I will, my dear," he promised. "And if you see me selling apples on a street corner, don't hesitate to come over and buy one."

He cradled the receiver and glanced up at the beamed ceiling of his den. "That confirms my suspicions about the Monarch mob," he said.

He got up, prowled around the room.

Back at the desk, he started to reach for the phone again. "I ought to call Frank up at that sylvan bordello he and Jane are visiting and inform him of this evening's exciting and thrill-packed events," he said. Then he shook his head. "Nope, they're probably deep in the arms of Morpheus. And why Frank lets that lout get in bed with the two of them is beyond me."

I think I can make it," said Jane, who'd managed to maneuver her chair close to one of the log walls of the cabin's living room.

My attempt to do something similar had been thwarted by a bearskin rug. At the moment I was becalmed at the edge of the damned thing, unable to wrestle my chair any farther. "Try," I urged. "I'll have to go around the bear."

"What the hell are you two morons doing?" asked Babs. "We're about to be cremated and you're staging a chair race."

Out in the kitchen the bloodhound was howling continuously and blackish smoke was already seeping in under the door from the front part of the wooden cabin we were trapped in.

"There's a chance," I said as I struggled to get the wood chair to hop sideways, "that we can tip over one of these chairs and get it to break. Then we can wiggle free of the ropes."

"You'll break your neck."

"Actually we're in a classic six-of-one-half-dozen-of-the-other situation, ma'am," I told her, making some small progress at circumventing the hairy rug. "A broken neck versus burning up in this cabin. Worth the risk."

"Bullshit," she observed.

"You might see if you can topple your chair," suggested Jane. She was close to the wall now and, straining, she got her feet to raise a few inches.

"Good," I said, watching her. "See if you can push against the wall."

She couldn't. But by rocking and twisting, she made the wooden chair bounce nearer to the wall. Then she was able to press her toes against one of the logs.

Jane bit her lip and pushed into the wall with her feet. Initially nothing happened.

Then the chair started to teeter.

"You got it, Jane."

"Wow," she said as the chair went falling over backward to smack hard on the floor.

The chair made some creaking noises when it smacked down. But it remained whole and Jane's bonds didn't loosen at all. "Damn it," she said.

"Let me see if I can do anything," I said.

"You'll never make it, schmuck," said Babs.

The smoke was getting thicker in the room and you could hear the fire burning its way through the room next to ours.

I speeded up my efforts and, all at once, a leg of the chair caught in a knothole in the wood floor.

There was a cracking and the chair and I tumbled over sideways. The stuck leg broke off completely as we went down and when the chair hit, the entire back of it collapsed.

For several seconds I remained sprawled on the floor, tangled up in ropes and broken wood. The sudden slamming hadn't done my headache much good and I felt dizzy.

"Frank, are you all right?"

"Yeah, fine." I disentangled myself and, very wobbly, stood up.

From my pants pocket I fished out a jackknife. Running to where Jane lay, I knelt and went to work on her ropes.

"You better hurry," advised Babs.

The wall behind her had just taken fire and the room was thick with smoke and crackling heat.

I got Jane cut loose, yanked away the strands of greasy rope and pulled her to her feet. "Can you walk?"

"Good enough to get the heck out of here."

I nodded at the kitchen door. "Gather up Dorgan and check the back door," I said. "Be careful, because some of those bastards may still be out there."

She gave me a very quick kiss on the cheek and hurried to the door that led to the kitchen.

"Am I just going to sit here and fry?" asked Babs.

I skirted the bearskin rug and got to her chair. "Sit still," I suggested and started slicing at the ropes that held her.

"Ouch," she said. "I'd like to come out of this with both arms, if you don't mind."

"Next time we'll have one of your servants come up with us and take care of saving your ungrateful ass," I said.

"That's no way to talk to me."

"Under the circumstances," I told her, getting the last of the ropes clear of her, "it seems very appropriate." I got a grip on her arm and tugged her up and free of the chair. "Let's go."

"Are they out there waiting to shoot us if we come barging out?"

"That's a possibility."

Jane was at the back door. She had it a few inches open and was looking out into the foggy dark. "No sign of anybody, Frank."

The bloodhound was pulling at the leash she held, scratching at the door.

The windows of the room we'd just been in exploded at that moment and a great gust of gray smoke came whooshing into the kitchen after us.

"Let's risk it," I said, edging around Jane.

I opened the door wider, scanned the silent night woods around the back of the burning cabin. I took a deep breath, feeling the way you do just before you head off the high board. Then I launched myself out and down the five wooden back steps.

Nothing happened.

I turned toward the door. "C'mon, it's okay."

Dorgan came galloping out, with Jane holding tight to his leash.

"You're sure it's not a trap?" asked Babs, framed in the doorway.

"If it is, ma'am, you make a terrific target, framed there like that."

"Asshole," she said and ran down to join us on the wet grass.

Jane had moved a few yards away from the cabin, which was burning fiercely now and sending flames and smoke up into the surrounding fog.

"Look over there by the little dirt road, Frank." She pointed.

I sprinted to her side. Parked at the side of the road was my yellow Plymouth coupe. "They must've moved it over here," I said. "To make it seem like I'd come here to this cabin of my own free will."

"Well, now we've got a way to get out of here before the woods takes fire."

"You mean all three of us are going to crowd into that dinky wreck?" asked Babs.

"Four," I corrected. "And it won't be so bad. You and Dorgan will have the rumbleseat all to yourselves."

Forty-two

The premiere of *The Pirate Prince* at Klein's Babylonian Movie Palace in the heart of Hollywood two nights later was memorable. They never did get around to showing the film, but that didn't seem to matter to most of the motion picture stars, newspaper columnists, fan magazine writers, studio executives and hangers-on who filled the ornate temple of the cinema on that particular evening.

The Babylonian is on Hollywood Boulevard, just down the block from Grauman's Chinese, and before the sun had even set on the movie capital, there were hundreds of people massed outside the theater awaiting the advent of the invited celebrities. As darkness hit Hollywood, a half-dozen huge spotlights snapped to life and shot bright white beams up into the sky.

Groucho was an old friend of Ira Klein and he had been able to wangle a few extra invitations. "I knew Klein in the days when he was part of a pantomime horse in vaudeville," Groucho had told me. "I realized he was destined for great things as soon as I noticed he was playing the front end of the horse."

Most of the fans and tourists didn't recognize them, but Vince Salermo, Shel Leverson and Benton McLaughlin were among those who came walking along the red carpet that led into the huge movie palace that night.

There was an eleven-piece orchestra, all decked out in tuxedos, sitting in the pit in front of the stage. They played an overture based on the score of *The Pirate Prince,* a flamboyant, swashbuckling composition. It had been written by Erich Wolfgang Korngold, borrowed by Eli Kurtzman from Warner Brothers at considerable expense.

At sixteen minutes after eight, which was sixteen minutes later than the scheduled time for commencing, Conrad Nagel stepped out onto the stage. The house lights dimmed and a single spot caught his slim figure, dapper in white tie and tails.

He bowed toward the box on his left that held Kurtzman, Jack Gardella and their wives. Nagel then smiled at the audience, singling out Claudette Colbert in one of the front rows and also nodding personally at Kay Francis. He approached closer to the microphone. "Ladies and gentlemen, on behalf of Mr. Eli Kurtzman and Monarch Pictures, it is my very great pleasure to welcome you here tonight to this marvelous temple of entertainment, Klein's Babylonian Movie Palace, for the world premiere of one of the greatest historical epics ever to come out of our wonderful town of Hollywood," he said. "I can assure you that Mr. Kurtzman has spared no expense to make absolutely certain that *The Pirate Prince* is authentic in every way and that, while faithful to the bloody history of the buccaneers who roamed the Spanish Main, it provides only wholesome entertainment for all the family."

Nagel paused, bowing again toward the Monarch box.

"I am sorry, on this auspicious occasion, to have to inform you that the brilliant star of *The Pirate Prince,* the gifted Tom Kerry, will not be able to attend tonight's event."

A disappointed sound came from the audience.

"Mr. Kerry, upon advice of his physician, is resting up after the rigors of performing so splendidly in the wonderful motion picture you're about to see this evening. On behalf of—"

That was as far as Nagel ever got.

Behind him the vast sequined curtain that hid the movie screen suddenly began to rise. And from the orchestra pit rose the strains of "Hurray for Captain Spalding."

Groucho, accompanied by a separate spotlight of his own, came slouching on stage. He held a fat cigar between his fingers and he had his trademark moustache painted on.

The master of ceremonies, who hadn't been expecting this intrusion, took a step back from the microphone. He frowned at the approaching Groucho, then smiled weakly and took two more steps to the rear.

Groucho's deep bow toward Kurtzman and Gardella in their box nearly caused him to topple off the stage. He managed to right himself just in time. From the edge of the stage he waved at some of the people he knew. "Claudette, you're going to have to start wearing lingerie if you persist in showing up in dresses like that."

With a lopsided shrug, he bounded over and took hold of the mike. "Ladies and gentlemen, and you, too, Conrad," he said, "I've been asked to present a special tribute to the late Tom Kerry. So, before you settle down to view this evening's masterpiece, *The Pirate Prince,* I'm going to—"

"Tom Kerry isn't dead," shouted Gardella from above. He was on his feet, clutching the edge of the box. "Get that idiot off the stage."

In the third row Vince Salermo stood up. "Let him finish his piece first, Jack," he suggested. He had his right hand thrust inside the jacket of his double-breasted gray suit.

The audience was talking, murmuring, whispering. The questions "What's he talking about?" and "Is Kerry dead?" were the ones most frequently heard all across the darkness of the huge theater.

"If you'll hush up now," requested Groucho, "I'll continue with my lecture." He gestured toward the projection booth. "If you would."

A slide was projected onto the vast sparkling movie screen. It was one of the publicity shots of Peg McMorrow.

"This is Peg McMorrow," said Groucho. "She was murdered a few days ago."

"Stop him," shouted Kurtzman. "He's ruining the premiere."

"Keep your mouth shut, Eli," called Salermo, who'd remained standing.

"Next," said Groucho quietly into the microphone.

What the audience now saw was a blowup of one of Peg's snapshots of Tom Kerry and Babs McLaughlin arguing in the woods near the Shadow Lodge.

"Three weekends ago," continued Groucho, "Peg Mc-

Morrow went up to Lake Sombra, a spot many of you are no doubt familiar with, in the company of Tom Kerry. While they were there, Kerry encountered an old girlfriend of his, Mrs. Babs McLaughlin. They—"

"That's enough, Groucho. I won't have you talking about my wife like this." Benton McLaughlin had left his seat in the middle of the house and was stalking down the aisle toward the stage.

One of Salermo's men eased up out of his chair and headed him off.

"Peg was suspicious and managed to take some snapshots of the two of them," Groucho said.

The audience was very quiet now.

"When she later read that Babs McLaughlin had supposedly disappeared down in Baja California, Peg suspected that something was wrong," continued Groucho. "She knew that Kerry had spent time with the woman and she thought that maybe he'd done her harm. She was damned certain the woman wasn't anywhere near Baja most of that particular weekend. Being more interested in furthering her career than in seeing justice done, Peg decided to sell her pictures to somebody. She couldn't find Kerry, which isn't too surprising. At that point he was buried under the sod up in the woods near Lake Sombra. His body isn't there anymore, of course, since that was only a temporary resting place anyway."

"He's crazy," shouted Gardella. "Stop him."

"We're getting close to the finale, Jack, be patient," suggested Groucho. "Now Peg was killed, and her death passed off as a suicide, to keep her from making public her pictures and her knowledge. Even though she was wrong about who'd been killed, they didn't want her going to the papers or the police with her accusations. There are, surprisingly enough, a few honest cops and reporters in Southern California and Peg just might've been able to reach one of them." Groucho looked up at the box. "Tom Kerry was the one who'd been killed. Babs McLaughlin had been a witness to the murder and she was being kept out of sight until they could figure out what to do with her. The man who killed Kerry out of jealousy was our old friend Eli Kurtzman."

That caused an enormous gasp from just about everybody inside the movie palace.

Kurtzman was on his feet now, glaring down at Groucho. "That's slander, you son of a bitch," he cried. "I'll drag your ass through every court in—"

"You're forgetting something, Eli," cut in Groucho. "There was a witness. You know damn well you don't have her anymore. In fact, your goons have been trying to find her for the past two days."

That was my cue. Jane and I had been in the wings, standing on each side of a very nervous and uneasy Babs McLaughlin. Ever since we'd returned from the lake with her, she'd been kept very quietly at a little hotel I knew about near Angel's Flight. We'd all met with Groucho as soon as we got back to L.A. He'd come up with this plan for confronting Kurtzman and Gardella. Using a lot of cajoling and promises of lucrative deals when she eventually told her story to the press for a large fee, Groucho persuaded Babs to agree to remain hidden until the premiere.

Now I escorted her out onto the stage. "Nothing to be

afraid of," I assured her as I led her right up to the microphone.

"In a pig's eye," she said. "But don't worry. I'll tell the whole damn story. It's about the only thing I can do to get myself out of this mess."

She only told part of it, voice shaky, body trembling.

Gardella had gone shoving out the back of the box to come down to the main floor of the theater. He started to climb up on the stage, intending to keep her from saying any more, I guess.

He never made it, though.

The husky troubleshooter was on the second plush-covered step when there were two shots. Both took him low in the back. He lurched to the right and, very briefly, rose up on his toes. Then he staggered to the left and dropped over into the orchestra pit.

The drummer jumped clear in time and the big man slammed into the kettledrum and died.

While just about everyone was watching that happen, there were two more shots.

Up in the Monarch box a woman screamed, a thin rattling scream. "Eli," she cried. "Eli."

A spotlight swung over and there was Kurtzman hanging over the edge of the box. There was a large bloody splotch where the slugs had come ripping out through his back.

By the time the police arrived and got around to looking, there wasn't a trace of Shel Leverson in the Babylonian Movie Palace. In fact, he didn't ever turn up again in Los Angeles. Groucho suggested that the gambler really had loved Peg McMorrow and revenged himself on the two men who'd arranged her death. I agree with that, although Leverson didn't strike me as the sentimental type.

While we were waiting for the police to arrive, I sat back-stage beside Jane.

McLaughlin had joined his wife and was promising her something about sticking by her. I didn't hear everything she said back to him, but the word *bullshit* occurred more than once.

Groucho was still out on stage, his legs dangling over the edge and every reporter and columnist who'd been at the pre-miere was trying to interview him. Flash bulbs were popping a lot, too.

After they got through with Groucho, some of them came back to talk to me.

One of my old colleagues from the *Times* nodded at Jane. "What's the young lady's relationship to you, Frank?"

I grinned. "She's my fiancée," I told him.

She leaned closer to me. "That's absolutely correct," she said.

The next evening the initial broadcast of our radio show went out from Studio F in the Nationwide Broadcasting Network building on Hollywood Boulevard.

The majority of news stories about Groucho's clearing up of the McMorrow-Kerry murders had mentioned the show. The client, the ad agency and the network were all very pleased.

At exactly six P.M. Pacific time Groucho, wearing a checked sport coat, tan slacks and a greasepaint moustache, stepped up to the mike.

The studio audience applauded on cue.

When the sound of that faded down, he said, "Good evening, this is Groucho Marx, and on behalf of Orem Brothers Coffee . . ." He paused, looking up at Jane and me in the booth and rolling his eyes. ". . . I want to welcome you to the very first broadcast of *Groucho Marx, Master Detective.*"